PROUDLY FLAWED

MEADE FISCHER
COPYRIGHT 2024
WWW.MEADEFISCHER.COM

Chapter 1

Heather wasn't convinced she wanted to be in this tedious little professional office. Her last experience with a therapist wasn't worth the time spent talking to a boring woman who seemed to only speak in canned phrases. This time, however, she was having some issues that had not come up in the past, so why not give it a try. This guy didn't look very impressive, but that's not why she was here. Also, she tended to judge a person by his space, and this office was bland, off-white walls, a comfortable, but boring brown chair for her, an office chair for him. A small table with a file placed just so on it, his diploma and professional association document on the wall, but nothing personal, nothing to say he was anything but bland.

"So, Heather, your mother Lisa referred you to therapy, and why is that?" He looked up from his notes to wait for her response.

"Well, she's not exactly my mom, more my adopted mom, but it's that I'm starting to have some guilt feelings about stuff that happened three years ago."

Sean Williams was a psychologist with a small private practice in Santa Monica, a man slipping gently into middle age, with a failed marriage, a daughter he rarely sees and a receding hairline. This girl, a high school senior was quite striking with her blond hair and flawless complexion.

"So what problem from three years ago is bothering you?"

"I'm not sure I can talk about it. It's actually rather criminal, and I don't want to go to jail, even though maybe I deserve it."

"Don't worry, Heather. This is doctor patient confidentiality. The only thing that would break that is if I felt you were about to harm yourself or others, but this being years ago, that wouldn't apply. In other words, anything you say to me is private."

"Okay doctor. I killed three boys when I was fourteen." She paused to let that sink in, and for a moment Sean didn't know what to say. This was said so nonchalantly that it was almost as unemotional as if she'd said, "nice office." When he recovered, he needed clarification. "How do you mean killed? Was it some accident or what?"

Heather moved in her chair, getting settled and comfortable while she carefully chose her words. Then she leaned forward, a gesture of confidentiality. "No, there were three boys, three dates, and I sort of murdered all three of them. That's how I met Lisa, she is the assistant district attorney, and she was going to put me in jail."

Sean mentally reeled from what the girl said. She had murdered three boys, and her adopted mother was going to send her to jail. She had his attention. "Perhaps you should tell me the whole story."

"I had some anger issues about guys in general, my dad also. I didn't like guys treating girls as if they were like second class citizens and all that, and these boys just pushed my buttons, so I killed them, and at the time I found it a sexual turn on, but no remorse." She followed that comment with a fleeting, weak smile.

"So, no remorse at the time, but you are feeling guilty now?"

"Yeah, my attitude about guys has changed since I became a dominate. Now I treat guys as if they belong to me, and I sort of want to protect them."

Sean realized that she was the first dominate female he'd met, and he found that fascinating, and he wanted to learn more. "So you have boys you dominate? And how did that phase of your life begin?"

"My fifteenth birthday. I was sort of dating this timid, shy boy who was like in awe of me or something. We were at dad's place in Montecito, and I was in the bedroom with this boy, and suddenly I got this idea. I ordered him to strip and get on the bed. He looked kind of panicky, but I insisted, and he obeyed. I loved the feeling of power, so I mounted him and had a great orgasm. It was then I knew what and who I was. So now it's both boys and men. Right now there's a boy from school and also a twenty-two year old guy. I like to have at least two submissives at any time, each serving me in a different way."

"So, having submissive guys changed your attitude, and you no longer have any desire to kill or harm them?"

"No. They belong to me, so I'm responsible for them. I'm strict but caring. My subs appreciate the way I treat them."

Sean found it interesting that she said they belonged to her, as if they were pets or articles of clothing. "What do submissive men do for you?"

"They do my bidding sexually, and they, you know, worship me, kiss my feet, all that kind of thing. I also enjoy pegging."

He wanted to know the details of the killings, so Heather paused, a look of pain on her face, before starting in. "Basic info or full account?"

"Basic should do for now. Go ahead."

"First one was showing off by standing on the edge at Pacific Palisades, daring me to join him. One little push and he went over the edge. The next, parked almost the same place. He was being a jerk, so I pretended I'd lost an earring, and while he looked for it on his knees, I put the car in gear and ran him over. The third guy was showing off his fishing knife and tried to get fresh with me, so I stabbed him in the heart. I also tried to kill my stupid lawyer, but that didn't go well. He survived with some injuries."

He was both listening and observing her. She related these killings with a minimum of emotion, perhaps a pained, almost introspective look, but little else. Being curious, and wanting to see more reactions, he pressed her for more details. He noticed a slight look of discomfort when she mentioned, almost offhandedly, that killing them was sexually arousing, causing her to masturbate.

The session time was running out, and Sean wanted to know if she was up for another session the following week. She agreed, and said he was better than the therapist she had three years ago. He also asked her if he could discuss any of this with Lisa. "I tend not to broadcast my domination and my subs, but mom pretty much knows what's going on, so no secrets. Go ahead and talk to her."

Heather got up, shook his hand, thanked him and casually walked out the door, with a slight swagger, leaving Sean rather perplexed. In the fifteen years he'd been treating patients, this was a totally new experience, and he wasn't exactly sure how to handle it. A conversation with the girl's mom would be helpful.

Lisa Carr was a pretty open person, a minimum of prejudices, but when she first found out about Heather's fetish, it bothered her, thinking about how she almost made slaves out of the guys she dated. It was Steve who put things in perspective, saying that his years working in film had exposed him to every type one might imagine, and while that lifestyle wasn't really common, it was common enough that he'd met several women who were dominate and who had subs, some actually professionals, with men paying for the privilege of being dominated. He also knew some submissive women who loved being dominated by men. The bottom line is that if it is consensual, even if weird, it was all part of being human.

Actually, as Lisa processed her new daughter's fetish, she realized that being dominate also meant she no longer had any urge to hurt males, and that seemed a good tradeoff.

That evening Sean called Lisa at home, said he'd had an interesting session with Heather and was wondering if Lisa could shed some light on a few things.

"Certainly. This is an important breakthrough, the guilt, and I think she's ready to face her past."

"Apparently you know about the domination thing?"

"Yes, and while it may sound weird to many people, I've discovered it's a rather popular kink, and, more importantly, it seems to have eliminated her homicidal tendencies. Besides, I made sure that she wasn't abusing her subs, that they were willing participants."

"What does your husband think?"

Lisa gave a short laugh. "Steve is a film actor, and he is exposed to every kink in the book. Nothing shocks him. He just wants Heather to use protection, you know, disease or getting pregnant."

"And does she use protection?"

"Yeah, she's a very responsible girl, very close to becoming a legal adult."

Sean wanted to know if Lisa knew about Heather's two subs, but Lisa said she tried not to know the details of her daughter's sex life.

"Next week we will go deeper, perhaps uncover something. I will keep you posted."

Steve had been away for over a week, working on a script and staying in Montecito, while Lisa's work and Heather's school were in Santa Monica. He had said he'd be coming to town tonight, so a family dinner for the first time in a couple weeks.

The family tradition is to have a small glass of wine with dinner, and even though Heather was not old enough to drink, Lisa felt that a bit of wine with dinner would satisfy Heather's curiosity, so he wouldn't be tempted to go out and get drunk.

Steve regaled them with his stories about the film, the crew and some of the funny incidents. Lisa noted the changes that had come over him in the three years they'd been together, how as he was now on the downhill side of his forties, how he was slowly giving way to middle age, rather than the guy she'd met who always tried to be younger and would never go out with a woman over thirty. She liked to think she'd somehow domesticated him, and he seemed more content with his new life.

Then Steve turned his attention to Heather. "It seems you have a new therapist. How did that go?"

"Good. I'm going to keep going in every week. He seems kind of nice, but I think I freaked him out." She laughed at that. She was wearing her standard uniform, faded, loose-fitting jeans and a tee shirt with a clever saying on it. This one said, "Diagonally parked in a parallel universe."

Lisa asked what she meant about the therapist being freaked out.

"When I told him I was a dominant and had subs, his eyes widened and his jaw kind of dropped. He recovered quickly, but it was obvious he'd never met anyone like me."

Steve laughed. "That right, because there isn't anyone else just like you. You are certainly one of a kind."

Heather smiled at Steve, taking his comment as a compliment. She had grown fond of him over these last three years, seeing beyond his macho act to the genuine guy, the one he'd never show at the studios. He really cared about her in his awkward way.

Steve had brought home some clips from the film he was shooting, and they all spent some time looking at them and commenting. Lisa said, "Steve, you are showing more depth with every film. I'd say you've really matured as an actor."

"Matured is just another name for growing old." He laughed somewhat uncomfortably.

School is hard for teens, as the schedule seems to be designed for older people, like teachers and staff, school starting far too early for the average kid. So, as much as she would have liked to stay up until well past midnight, Heather excused herself at 10 and went to bed, the glass of wine helping her to relax.

Steve, watching her leave the room, said, "Next year she'll be off to college, and I think we're both going to miss her."

"Yeah, the daughter we never had; the daughter we learned to love."

The next day at school, her sub, Tommy, seeing an opportunity, whispered in her ear. "Does Mistress want me to come over after school to serve her?"

"That won't work. Steve is home, and it would be awkward."

"Would Mistress like to come to my place? My parents don't get home until after six."

"I will think about it sub and let you know." Then she turned and walked away, leaving Tommy standing there like an abandoned puppy.

She wasn't fond of Tommy's place, and she was in the mood for the kind of oral sex she always got from Kirk, her twenty-two year old sub. She wouldn't bother saying anything to Tommy, knowing that a simple no would not be questioned.

At lunch, she called Kirk. "Hi sub. I'd like to enjoy you this afternoon, right after school. I assume you are free?"

"Of course Mistress. I'm always free for you. I'm working from home, so any time would be wonderful."

"Good boy. I've trained you well. See you later."

Heather always insisted her subs called her Mistress, a gesture of respect and obedience.

After school Heather hopped on the little scooter

Steve had bought for her, and she headed over to Kirk's apartment. Kirk Dallas was a tall, thin young man who did accounting work, often from home. His small apartment, a sign that he didn't make much money, held his work space and his bedroom and little else. There were a couple of chairs in front of the TV and a small kitchen. Since he'd become Heather's sub, he had been far more meticulous about keeping his house clean and neat. Once she'd come over, discovered that his toilet had a ring, slapped him and then left. He had learned his lesson. He had not been very successful with women until Heather touched the submissive he'd denied for years. This new realization was liberating, and serving heather, kissing her feet, giving her oral sex, letting her peg him. He found it really exciting when she had him kneeling naked, masturbating for her enjoyment.

As soon as she walked in the door she said, "I have to inspect your place sub, and if it is clean enough, I'll amuse myself with you."

Kirk stepped aside, and Heather walked around the tiny apartment, deciding he'd cleaned it well enough. Then she turned to him, shook her head and said, "Why is my sub still clothed? You know I want you naked."

Kirk quickly pulled off his clothes and stood there for her inspection, already getting an erection.

She approached him, grabbed his cock and started to massage it, and just as he was getting ready to ejaculate, she stopped and slapped it hard, causing him to cry out in pain. "Not yet sub. You haven't earned it yet. I need you to very carefully undress me and service me."

Kirk knew the routine, and he did it all exactly as she'd trained him. Only when she was satisfied did she allow him to masturbate for her. Then she got dressed and patted him on the head, calling him a good boy, and then headed home.

Heather got home shortly before Lisa, Steve had already gone out to meet someone from the studio. She fixed dinner, something she loved to do for Lisa, opened a bottle of wine and poured one for Lisa, a short one for herself and set the table.

There was a table right by the front door, and Lisa, without fail, would always throw her briefcase on it, kick off her shoes and let out a deep sigh. "Home at last. How was your day sweetie?"

"Nothing special. Good math class, and I stopped by Kirk's place for a few minutes on the way home."

"And how is your young man?"

"He's okay, but I'm starting to get a bit bored with him."

Lisa settled into a chair, picked up her glass of wine and said, "I used to get bored with men after awhile, at least until I got together with Steve. You'll find the right partner soon enough, hopefully after you finish college. Which reminds me, how are the enrollment opportunities? Any decisions?"

"I was thinking of UCLA. I could save the cost of a dorm and just live here."

"I'd love that, but part of the college experience is living on campus, getting involved in all that."

She paused for a bit, deep in thought. "I'm not sure how I feel about that. I don't think I fit into the usual social groups and all that."

"You're almost a legal adult, and I trust your judgment. Just make sure you don't hurt anyone."

"Oh, Mom. I'm so over that. Now that I understand how weak and needy guys are, I only want to take care of them and train them. Will Steve be home tonight?"

"I think so, his meeting was here in town, so doubt he'd head to Montecito."

Since Steve always eats at his meetings, Lisa and Heather sat down to eat, have a glass of wine and conversation. Heather always loved to hear about Lisa's day and the strange people she had to prosecute, most of whom were criminals simply because they were too damn stupid to earn a living any other way. Lisa's way of telling her daily stories were always humorous, since she'd learned to no longer let them bother her. Prosecuting these guys was almost fun, hearing their bizarre stories and lame excuses.

As Lisa was picking up the dishes and putting them in the dishwasher, she remembered something. "Still good with that therapist?"

"Yeah. Really helps to talk about it, sort it out and all. I'm only afraid I will start to cry."

"Crying is fine sweetie. It's not a sign of weakness." However, Lisa realized that to Heather crying was a sign of weakness. What others see as the girl's strength, Lisa saw as a desperate attempt to stay in control, and that was one of the reasons she understood her daughter's lifestyle.

Heather was watching Nature on PBS when Steve walked in. "Nature again. I think my little girl is going to be a biologist or ecologist. Mind if I join you?" Steve's rhetorical question didn't wait for an answer before he dropped into an easy chair.

After the show ended, Heather asked a question that had been on her mind for awhile. "Steve, I never hear you comment on my dominant lifestyle, so I don't know if you disapprove."

Steve turned off the TV and turned to Heather. "I neither approve or disapprove. Your life is your life, and as long as you aren't hurting yourself or anyone else, I have no right to comment or form an opinion."

"Women dominating men doesn't bother you?"

"Let me tell you about this woman in the editing department. She's a dominant, actually a dominatrix, and her thing is handcuffs and whips, so you are pretty innocuous, almost vanilla." He chuckled a bit about the vanilla part.

"I think whips and handcuffs are too weird. I just like guys who obey my orders."

A few days later Lisa got a call from Tommy's mother. "Your daughter made my boy give her money for something she wanted, and I want that to stop."

"She can't make him do anything. He's bigger than her, and he's free to refuse. If he wants to spend his money on her, if it's his money, it's his decision."

That didn't satisfy the woman, but left her with little recourse. Lisa was no fan of her daughter's lifestyle, but she'd been with enough men to know that many love to buy women gifts to win their favor. Sexual selection. Male birds use bright feathers to attract and convince females, human males use money. Lisa had let men buy her things when she was a broke student, but once she started earning good money, she stopped that, wanting to have a level playing field in her romantic relationships.

The one household rule was that Heather couldn't bring any subs home when Lisa or Steve were home. Sanctity of the home was the rationale.

Sean wanted to learn as much as possible about this dominant thing before meeting with Heather again, so he did some research, learning that it was not uncommon and actually a growing trend, as men abandoned their traditional roles and women gained ground in education and careers. Some men fantasized about being dominated, but didn't act on it until some woman gave him a little push in that direction, after which the man would fall fully into it. Apparently it took a woman who could spot that tendency in a man and who knew how to cultivate it, a woman with a seriously dominant mindset.

"Do I call you doctor or Mr. Williams or Sean?"

"You can call me Sean if you are comfortable with that Heather."

"Okay, Sean, the more I think about killing those boys, the more, I guess you would call it, guilt I'm feeling, and I don't like that feeling."

"That's understandable. You can't bring those boys back, and you can only guess as to how they might have turned out. However guilt is your mind's way of processing it and making you understand that it was wrong, that you had serious issues, and that being very young, you didn't know how to deal with them properly. You can't excuse your behavior, but you can understand it, own it and move on with your life. There may come a time for an emotional catharsis, tears, regrets and all that. It's part of the process, and when it comes, embrace it."

"You're right about one thing; I can't bring them back, and for a long time I thought that they were jerks and deserved it, but I don't think anyone deserves to be murdered."

"Heather, I think we can both agree on that. I would suggest that when you are ready for that emotional catharsis, your adopted mother would be the safe person to have that with."

"Yeah, she'd be the only one I could ever cry around."

When Heather told Lisa about that discussion, Lisa confirmed that she would always be a safe place for Heather to express her feelings, a non-judgmental place, even though Lisa doubted she could be totally non-judgmental about murder.

Chapter 2

It was winter break for Heather. Steve wasn't filming, so his time was his own, and Lisa always took some vacation time around the holidays. They decided to go to Hawaii, get a hotel on Waikiki beach. After unpacking Heather put on her bathing suit and walked to the beach. A young man came up and tried hitting on her, giving her his best lines and pouring on the charm. She just stared at him until he started to feel uncomfortable. Then she said, "Do you want to date me?"

Her directness set him back for a moment, and he recovered and said yes, he would like that.

She said, "Sit down. I don't like looking up at people."

He sat down, and she looked at him as if he were a meal she was about to eat. "You need to know that I'm a dominant woman, and I would expect you to obey me at all times. Do you think you could do that?"

The guy was stuck for a few seconds, not knowing what to say, never having been in a situation like this before. "I don't know about that. It isn't what I expected to hear."

"Two choices, agree to obey or leave me alone. I'm busy, so decide quickly."

She could see that she had touched something that he was uncomfortable with, but she wouldn't let him off the hook. She just kept looking right into his eyes, making him uncomfortable. After a minute and quite conflicted, the guy got up, excused himself and started to walk away.

"Wait. What's your name?"

He stopped and turned back. "Tim."

"I think I'd like to call you Timmy. Can you handle that?"

"Yeah, sure, I guess." And since she didn't say anything else, Tim walked away.

That was close, she thought. He almost caved, and I love it. This encounter put her in an adventurous mood, so She walked to the rental stand and rented a surfboard, the waves at Waikiki Beach were considered perfect for beginners.

After falling off the board several times, she caught the attention of a surfer near by, and he suggested that perhaps he could help. Why not, she thought, so "sure, I could use some help."

He explained about centering herself on the board and as soon as the wave started to propel her, how to get her feet under her and get up without falling. A few more trys, and she was able to get up and get a short ride. She wondered if the guy was going to try to make time with her, but he seemed content to help and get back to his own surfing. Pity, she thought. He might have been fun.

Tim was running over the conversation he'd had with the girl, wondering why her attitude was exciting him, wondering how it would feel to obey a girl, to do what she says. Part of him thought that guys didn't do that, while another part let him fantasize about it, slipping gently down the rabbit hole of submission. Try as he might, Tim couldn't get her out of his mind, and being called Timmy made him feel like a boy, rather than a man, and this by a girl probably younger than him.

The next day Steve rented a car, and the family explored the north shore and waves Heather wouldn't consider messing with. After exploring and going to the botanical garden, they got back in time for her to hit the beach again.

After settling in on the beach, suddenly she was in the shade, so she opened her eyes to see a young man standing over her. "Yes, can I help you?"

"Don't you remember me?"

"No. Should I?"

"My name is Tim, Timmy. Yesterday we met and you wanted me to obey you, but I left."

"Okay, now I remember. So, are you ready to obey?"

"I dunno, maybe."

"Make up your mind, and while you are thinking, I expect to be called Mistress."

That seemed to push him over the edge. "Yes

Mistress."

"Good boy. Now sit down and tell me about yourself."

He was a twenty-one-year-old college student who had saved up for a week on the beach, and he was lonesome and hoped they could spend some time together.

"Now ask me properly, and maybe we can do something."

It took him a moment to put it together, but he was a quick study. "Mistress, I would like to spend time with you and obey your orders."

"Good boy. Now you can buy me a glass of wine."

He rushed over to the bar on the beach, got two glasses of wine, first showing his ID, and came back and offered one to her.

"You know I'm not old enough to drink, so good thing you went for the drinks."

"So, how old is Mistress?"

"Seventeen, but birthday coming up soon. I have plans with my parents tonight, but I will allow you to take me to lunch tomorrow. You will meet me here at noon. Do you understand?"

"Yes Mistress, noon tomorrow, right here."

"Don't be late, and you may now run along."

"Yes Mistress." He got up, excused himself and walked away.

It's getting easier all the time, she thought. Males cave in the presence of a dominant female, at least many of them do. The rest are unimportant and not worth bothering with. She slipped her hand into her bathing suit and started to stimulate herself, realizing that no one else on the beach was paying any attention to her.

That evening over dinner at one of those Hawaiian Luau places, Heather casually said, "Met some guy on the beach today. He's taking me to lunch tomorrow, so will I miss something?"

"Be back by 2 please. We have plans to hike up Diamond Head. Is it just lunch?" Lisa was asking.

"Just lunch, and yes, I'll be back. Looking forward to hiking with you guys."

The next day, noon exactly, Timmy walked up and said, "Mistress, I don't even know your name."

"Just call me Mistress Heather. Do you have a good place for us to eat? And by the way, parents have plans for us at 2."

Timmy was obviously disappointed, thinking that this might lead to something more intimate, but he was in too deep now, so he said, "Okay, I guess we'd better hurry."

Timmy was obviously uncomfortable over lunch, trying to make conversation with a girl who made him very nervous and who stared into his eyes, saying little. It was clear to Heather than Timmy was glad that she had to go, not knowing what might happen. She had left him rethinking his ideas about the relationship between men and women.

Heather stopped thinking about Timmy as soon as she left the restaurant. She discovered, much to her discomfort, that she was winded going up those long stairs to the top of Diamond Head, noticing that Lisa took it in her stride. Damn, she thought, mom's middle aged and in better shape. She vowed to start jogging soon. Steve, in an attempt to show he was still the young stud, ran up the stairs, at least until he was out of sight of Heather and Lisa, panting heavily by the time he reached the top.

It was time to end winter break, to go back to work, to school, to making movies, and they reluctantly said goodbye to Hawaii.

Back home, Heather found some one on one time with Lisa, on the patio, with the morning mist starting to dissipate, and asked her if she thought getting guys to buy lunch without giving them anything in return was selfish or wrong.

"Honey, men are always trying to impress women, buying them drinks, meals and all that. We have no obligation to do anything but be good company. You know I stopped doing all that when I started making a good income. I wanted a level playing field with men, equality and all that." Lisa realized that Heather would soon be starting a career and would be an independent woman with an income, not dependent on any man.

"I don't think I like the equality thing mom. I'm only comfortable when I'm in charge, in control. I never want to feel a guy is my equal. Makes me feel somehow weak."

"Sure, and I've had guys who wanted to give me control, and it was kind of fun, but really not my thing. We are all different, and as long as you and the boys are okay with the arrangement, I guess pretty much anything goes. I hope you aren't into inflicting pain."

"Never. Boys give me control, so I have to take care of them, protect them, you know?"

"Good that you are not extreme in this fetish. I sense that you want my approval, and yes, I approve of your lifestyle. I think it has solved the problem you had."

"You mean being a killer. Yeah, once they surrender to me, I have no desire to hurt them."

Lisa laughed at the idea of Heather needing to protect men, but then said, "Remember they are people, not pets."

With a big grin, Heather responded, "What if they like being pets?"

Lisa had enough experiences with men to relate to what Heather was saying, thinking of all the men she'd known who were basically looking for a mother.

"Well, as long as they aren't literal pets." The two women laughed about this, about how men can be and how they can be treated.

Chapter 3

Heather's relationship to men had changed since she was a freshman, a fourteen year-old, but one thing hadn't changed, the reality that she had no female friends outside of Lisa, who was more mom than friend. She used to take pride in this, that she didn't need to waste her time with the silly girls at school, but lately she had started to see things differently, had started to feel something was missing. She would have liked to have some female friends, but she had no idea how to start a friendship. As luck would have it, another girl broke the ice with her, a girl in one of her classes.

"Heather, right? I'm Julie."

Heather was aware of the girl. There was something about her that made Heather
Curious, but she couldn't put her finger on it. "Yeah, Julie, I know who you are."

"I've been watching your interaction with Tommy, and I get the impression that he might be your submissive."

Heather's red flag went up. She always thought she'd been circumspect, low profile about her kink, but this girl, almost a stranger, had somehow picked up on it.

"What gives you that idea, and why do you want to know about Tommy and me?"

Heather's defensiveness was obvious, and the other girl smiled and said, "Don't worry. I'm a dominant too. My boyfriend is my submissive, and I control him. I think we might be the only doms in this school, so perhaps we could be friends."

Heather took her time responding, considering everything involved in admitting to her fetish. This Julie was even taller than Heather, who was five-eight and still growing. Julie must have been an inch or two taller and more heavily built. She had short, brown hair and a nice, open face. She was torn, one part of her wanted to have another person to talk about her lifestyle, and another part that wanted to keep others at arms length. Julie's open smile helped Heather relax and do something uncharacteristic, open up. "Yeah, Tommy is my sub, one of them."

"Cool, you have others?"

"Have a twenty-two year old guy in town, mostly to please me sexually." Heather could hardly believe she'd just admitted that.

"Interesting. I haven't branched out like that yet, but maybe I will. Any problem keeping them balanced?"

Heather was starting to feel at ease, and she looked around to see if anyone was near enough to hear, but the class was over and the rest of the students had left for lunch. "No problem. They both know their place, and there's no overlap. Having at least two means you don't get dependent on any one guy."

"I hear that, girlfriend. You have it going on."

The term girlfriend, while not literally the case, somehow made Heather feel better. She was starting to like Julie. "Well, I've been at it for awhile. Got my first sub on my fifteenth birthday. Long story."

"Fine, you can tell me about it over lunch." The two girls walked out of the room and into a budding friendship.

Heather was doing homework on her computer when Lisa came home and saw the excited look on the girl's face. "Looks like someone had a good day."

"Yeah, mom. I think I made a new friend, my first female friend ever."

"Hold that thought while I put my briefcase away and pour a glass of wine."

Lisa listened while Heather told her all about Julie and all they have in common, favorite sports as well as being dominant women. They actually, Heather added, like the same TV shows.

Lisa was happy to hear that Heather had made a friend. She could become a fairly normal woman at this rate. Lisa recalled that as a freshman, Heather took pride in not making friends with all those "silly girls" at school. So much of that anger seems to have dissipated lately, and now with this new friend, Heather no longer seemed to feel like she was the total outsider.

The two girls started having lunch together daily, even telling their subs to stay away, to not interfere with "girl time."

Then came the day when Heather asked if she could have Julie over for dinner, to which Lisa agreed and said she'd fix something special for the girls. Steve said he'd be sure to be home for that dinner, that he'd reschedule other meetings and shootings.

Apparently, Heather hadn't bothered to tell Julie that her "dad" was a famous movie star, and Julie was totally stunned when she walked in to find Steve Longwood chopping onions in an apron. "OMG" the girl exclaimed. Steve Longwood?

'That's me. I'd shake your hand, but mine are rather covered in onion at the moment. Sit down and tell me about yourself."

It took the girl a few moments to regain her composure, and then she wanted to know how a movie star got to be Heather's step father.

"Lisa took on the chore of raising Heather, and I took on the chore of being Lisa's husband, so Heather rather came with the deal. She's a good kid in spite of her kinky lifestyle."

"So, you know about that?" Julie was a bit hesitant, knowing how many people disapprove.

"Oh yeah, and apparently you two share that lifestyle. Well, now you both have company."

"It doesn't bother you?"

"Global climate change bothers me; corrupt officials bother me; poverty bothers me, but people's sexual proclivities are not something I stress over. If you girls are happy, and your guys are happy, than what the hell. Do your parents allow you to have a glass of wine?"

"Yeah, with dinner."

Steve pulled a hand away from the onions and pointed to the refrigerator. "Open it up and pour yourself a small glass."

The girl was star-struck. A famous movie star was helping prepare dinner and had allowed her to have some wine. She could hardly wait to tell her mom, the woman who had introduced her to being a dominant. Julie had learned from and had taken after her dominatrix mother.

Julie was curious about the life of a movie star and had one question after another, all of which Steve was happy to answer, and at one point noting, "It's not all the pages of People Magazine. It can be hard work at times, particularly the more serious roles I seem to be doing these days."

Just then Heather walked in. "Hi dad. Working your charm on my friend?"

"He sure was." Julie said, "And I'm enjoying it."

"Heather, Julie is a delight. Hope you bring her around more often."

"You mean it?" Julie asked.

"Young lady, I mean everything I say, unless it's in front of a camera. Now, why don't you two run along, so I can finish up here. Lisa will be unhappy if I don't get these onions chopped."

The girls walked into the living room and sat down. "Is Steve Lisa's sub?"

"No, they have what's called an equal relationship, but there are things she insists on, and Steve respects that."

"It would be really cool if a famous movie star was her sub."

"Mom and I have had this conversation. Being a dominant isn't something she wants. She's into this equal relationship thing. Like, even though Steve makes way more money, she insists on paying half of everything they do."

"My sub pays for everything, and I like it that way."

"Yeah, me too, but everyone's different."

Lisa and Steve relaxed the wine requirement, allowing the girls to each have two with dinner. Then when Julie wanted to leave, Lisa said no. "I know it's only two glasses of wine, but I can't let you drive. I'll call your mother and say you are spending the night."

Julie realized that Lisa was a strong-willed woman, and she wasn't going to change her mind, so she nodded yes, and Lisa got on the phone, introducing herself to Julie's mom and saying she would like Julie to stay over rather than driving home late at night. Julie's mom seemed to agree, as Lisa said that it's a done deal.

That night in Heather's fortunately large enough

bed, she squeezed Julie's hand and said, "I've never had a best friend before."

"Well, you got one now, and I expect you to not cheat on me." With that they both laughed, said goodnight and turned off the lights.

In the morning, over coffee and breakfast in the sunny patio, Julie asked Heather about her real parents. "it isn't something I like to think about, but, okay. My dad, in a deep depression, took his life, and my mom is a raving drunk. I haven't heard from her in almost three years. Steve and Lisa are my family now."

"Wow, Heather. That's sad. At least I have my mom. My biological father left us when I was eight, and I was really sad about that for a long time, but when mom remarried, I learned to think of him as dad."

Chapter 4

Heather had a new attitude as she walked into school. No longer the invisible outsider, she had subs and a best friend, and she was someone, and she could hold up her head proudly, confidently. Her new confidence was noticed, and other students started talking with her, being friendly if not actual friends, which was pretty much how she wanted it. Some of the students actually knew her name. I'm not going to end up like either my mother or father, she thought. They were weak, but I'm strong. Nothing can hurt me.

Tommy, although hesitantly, ventured that Mistress seemed more confident and content. "Thank you for noticing sub. I like that you pay attention to your mistress. You are in the process of earning a reward."

To Tommy, a reward meant he would be allowed an orgasm, and he was looking forward to it. He didn't remember when Heather had taken total control of his orgasms, but he found that he couldn't cum without her permission, even if he tried, so he was now dependent on her good will, and he was always anxious to please, to earn favor.

Heather had learned through trial and error how often to give her subs a reward. Too often and they start to take it for granted, too seldom and they are less motivated to be good boys. Heather finally settled on every two weeks. It gave her subs something to look forward to, and it reminded them that it was a reward, which can be given or withheld, depending on Heather's mood. They were highly motivated to serve her.

She had discovered that boys and men responded very well to reward and punishment, that their pleasure was dependent on pleasing her. She always made sure her subs were well trained and would not do anything to displease her.

Naturally, Heather and Julie compared notes, now that they had a comfortable friendship, and Heather found out that Julie and her treated their subs pretty much the same. They had both researched female domination, so they knew what most did behind closed doors, and neither one was too outlandish. They didn't make their subs wear women's underwear, and they didn't do anything kinky in public, unlike some doms who actually walked their subs in public with a dog collar.

Sean Williams noticed the subtle changes in Heather, her more confident, more comfortable attitude. "Something has changed in your life. Would you like to talk about it?"

"I have a new friend, a best friend, my absolute first, and we have so much in common."

"As in what, favorite classes, sports, whatever?"

"We do have some of that in common, but turns out we are both dominant, and we both have loyal subs."

Sean noticed that Heather was dressing a bit differently. He jeans were less loose, and instead of old tee shirts, she was wearing nice tops, loose, comfortable but more stylish.

"You will be graduating soon Heather. What are your plans after that?"

"Both mom and Steve want me to go to college, and I think I want that too. I have good grades, so shouldn't be a problem. I'm thinking of UCLA, so I can be near my family."

Sean looked at her for a few moments before answering. "Interesting. So many students want to go away to school, to be more independent."

"Maybe they've had their family for their whole lives, so fine to go away. My family is less than three years old, and I'm still amazed at how lucky I've been. I don't want to go away, and I don't want them to forget about me." She suddenly stopped, realizing she'd said something she hadn't expected to say, something that came from deep inside. She wished she could take it back, but it was out there, and it was clear the psychologist was processing it, and she felt she'd shown a weakness.

"I see. It's like you can't believe your good

luck, and you don't want to jinx it."

Heather squirmed in her chair and looked out the window as if some bird on the wing would tell her what to say. "Yeah, I guess it's something like that. I don't want you to tell mom about that."

"Natually. Nothing we say goes past this room unless you wish it. Now what about the guilt feelings?"

"When I'm hanging out with Julie or playing with my subs, I sometimes stop thinking about all that. It doesn't seem as important then, and I guess that means I'm a bad person. I mean, I should feel bad about it all the time."

"Not really. No one feels bad about past mistakes all the time. You are not a bad person, just one with some issues that you are working on, trying to resolve."

"I think I was bad when I masturbated after seeing those boys dead. I regret that. I must have been a mental case."

"That you regret it is a sign you are dealing with it, working on resolving it. Progress Heather, real progress."

This guy was good, Heather thought as she left his office. She usually took the bus home, considering the parking situation in downtown Santa Monica, but this day she felt like walking the three miles home. It was a lovely late winter or early spring day, and there had been some fog in the morning, leaving just a hint of mist in the air, and it felt good and cool when she inhaled.

As she walked, she passed a guy, maybe a bit older than her, who turned to look at her. She fixed a strong gaze on him, making him uncomfortable, making him turn away. Another potential sub, she thought. The world is full of them. I'll never run out. She loved that she could intimidate guys with a look, a look she'd practiced until she could make men squirm when she gave them her strong, piercing gaze. She discovered that most people don't like to make prolonged eye contact, and that people would almost always turn away when she stared directly into their eyes.

Heather and Julie often speculated about whether there were other dominant girls in school, and they discussed how they might determine that without outright asking. They were certain that, in a school with over a thousand students, there must be at least one more dominant girl, and it would be fun to have more friends.

Both girls realized what a nightmare it would be if the school knew about their lifestyle. Life at school would become unbearable. They would have to come up with something that only another dominant would recognize and understand, but what? That gave them a project, a puzzle to solve, and they would spend some time each day working on it.

"We are two very smart women, so we can do this," Julie said.

They also discovered that their eighteenth birthdays were less than two weeks apart, so a big celebration, complete with loyal subs to serve them. Heather wondered if she could put both of her subs together at the same time. The idea was exciting, but it could be a total disaster. She would have to consider her options.

Chapter 5

It was interesting that her talks with the psychologist were actually being helpful, and it was mostly her doing the talking, with him reassuring her that she was actually not a bad person, rather a troubled person, a young woman with flaws and issues and all that. Young woman with issues sounds much better than evil killer, which is what she considered herself as she curled up in bed at night, allowing the darkness within and without to invade her heart and mind. This guy was being helpful, and she really owed mom for making this happen. Some day she was going to do something to make mom really proud of her.

Heather wasn't used to being vulnerable, but she wanted to tell Sean that she appreciated what he'd done. How could she do that while keeping her sense of control?

On her next session, Heather said, "I think you are good therapist, and you have helped me. I appreciate that."

That was a huge admission for Heather, and she waited for his response, hoping she hadn't given up too much.

"Thank you Heather. Believe it or not, this usually is a thankless job. People get better, but since I'm being paid, they don't always feel they need to thank me. Like you, I sometimes need positive feedback."

Wow, Heather thought. He's also vulnerable. For a moment she thought about having him for a sub, but she realized how fucking unprofessional that would be. Did she think she could make a sub of him? Probably not, him being a psychologist and all that crap.

Her final quarter as a high school student, with term papers and tests and getting the cap and gown and announcements, which she didn't think she needed, but

Lisa insisted on, saying she was going to invite all their mutual friends, which meant mostly Lisa's friends, who Heather thought, simply tolerated her for Lisa's sake. It was funny that she felt confident when dealing with males, but intimidated by other females, perhaps because she felt they could see through her, see that she wasn't what she appeared to be.

Maybe, Heather thought, that this whole graduation thing with guests and all that wasn't so bad after all. Lisa would probably invite Megan and D'Wanda. Heather hadn't seen them for some time, mostly because they were busy turning a few small restaurants into some kind of ass kicking chain with a new restaurant every six months. She liked those two women. They knew all about her but didn't judge her.

Heather was at her computer, trying to wade through her term paper when the phone rang. "Yo, Julie, what's up?"

"Just wanted you to know. I took a page from your book and got a second sub, and it more than doubled my pleasure."

"Cool. Are you going to let me meet him?"

"Yeah, but not sure yet if I'll share. Thinking like a scientist here. Maybe I'll keep adding subs until I discover the optimum number."

Heather hit save, smiled and said, "Great. Let's see if we both have the same optimum number. Perhaps we can publish our results in some kink magazine."

They both laughed at the idea of being researchers in the dom world. Perhaps, Heather thought, the two of them could start a magazine or a blog or something cool.

Lisa stuck her head into Heather's room. "Excuse me. Looks like you are working. Just wanted to say we've been invited to Steve's place this weekend, and you can bring a date, just one. Megan and D'Wanda will also come by, maybe stay over."

"Perfect. I'll bring my laptop and maybe get some of this paper done. Maybe my brilliant mom will give me a hand."

"I'm an officer of the court. I can't help you cheat, but good try."

As soon as Lisa closed the door, leaving Heather alone with her blinking cursor, she slipped into a daydream, thinking about how much Lisa had changed her, perhaps even saved, her life. She couldn't love her more if she were her real mother. And Steve was almost a father to her. I don't deserve this good fortune, she thought, but I will do everything I can to be deserving.

Chapter 6

Sean Williams was having coffee with another counselor, and they were, as they often did, discussing their cases, being careful not to mention any names. "I have a first for me. There's the seventeen-year-old girl who is a dominatrix, has two subs and is matter of fact about it, as if were the most normal thing in the world."

"Wow," Jay responded. "Seventeen is pretty young for that lifestyle." Jay was perhaps five or so years younger than Sean, but taller and quite thin, with hair that promised baldness by forty.

"Yeah, but she got her first sub on her fifteenth birthday, so she's pretty experienced by now."

"Are you judgmental at all about this?"

"Surprisingly no. The whole thing just fascinates me."

"Remember the basic rule here."

"Right," Sean replied. "No getting emotionally involved in her life."

"Sean, you know this might be a good one to write up."

"Sure, but after I see how it comes out. Her sexuality isn't her issue. She'd killed some boys a few years back."

"Oh, yeah. Fourteen-year-old, three boys dead, DA couldn't pin anything on her. That's your client?"

Sean admitted it was, but said not to share a word. Jay said Sean should certainly write this up. "Very unusual case. Probably neither of us will have another in our entire careers."

Sean took his friend's advice to heart and started putting his notes into a narrative, and the more he wrote, the deeper he went into the girl's psyche. I have to know what makes her tick, he thought. He called up an author he knew, an older guy who went by the name

"Sage," and asked his opinion and possibly his help.

"If you really want to understand her, maybe you should be her sub, first hand info."

"That's crazy. You know I can't do that."

"introduce us. Maybe I'll become her sub and perhaps a book will come out of it."

"Are you fucking serious?"

"Not sure, but it sounds like a fascinating idea. Think about it."

At their next session, Heather told him about Julie adding a sub, and them wondering what the optimum number was, maybe doing an experiment.

"That's a very clinical way of looking at it. Reminds me of a writer friend of mine who said he'd like to be a sub to learn about it and maybe write a book."

Heather perked up at that. "Really. Tell me about this guy. Like what's he look like and how old?"

"Tall, rather good looking. Looks young for someone around sixty. Why? You aren't considering..."

"Sure. Older guy, writer. He sounds like fun. Please introduce us."

"I'll have to think about that. You are still under age."

"Eighteen in one month. I really mean it. Introduce us, and I promise I won't take him for a sub until my birthday."

"I don't know about that. It doesn't sound like a good idea."

Heather stood up, so she could look down on him, put her fists on her hips and said, "You brought this up, and your friend wants to do it, so you've gotta do this for both him and me."

This was the first time he realized what a forceful personality the girl had, and it was rather intimidating. "I'll give him your message and your birthday, and then you two can do whatever you wish without me involved."

"Deal. Thank you."

When Sean told Sage-and he couldn't even remember the guy's real name- about what the girl said, the response was, "Fine, I'll contact her on her birthday."

"Just to warn you. You may be getting in over your head. Don't let her youth fool you."

"I'll take my chances. I'm not going to become

some teen girl's slave or anything like that."

What possessed me to do that, Sean thought. Perhaps morbid curiosity. I would, he thought, expect Sage to keep me informed about the details. This could be one for the journals.

Sage wrote down the girls number and her birthday, and started to think about the book that could come out of this, a first person account. It might involve some fun, kinky sex. Sounds like a win-win to me, he thought.

Heather told Julie about the possible older writer she might get for a sub. Julie said that Heather would definitely need to share that one with her.

The two girls went on some of the female lead relationships websites, lied about their ages, signed up and asked if there were any other dominant females in the Santa Monica area. Within a few days, they got several responses, mostly older women, but one popped up that got their attention. The girl alluded to being a student, but didn't specify high school or college, so they sent her a note, saying they were high school seniors and dominants.

It was hard to wait for a response, but they guessed the girl was trying to be careful, but after two days she responded that she was also a high school student, a sixteen year old junior, and it appeared that she was at their school. They sent her a message saying where they had lunch, along with a brief description of them, and then waited for a response.

The girls were enjoying-if anyone could actually enjoy school food- lunch, when a very attractive, dark skinned girl, clearly mixed race, walked up. "Heather and Julie?"

They got up, shook her hand and asked her to join them. "My name is Nadia, I'm originally from India. We moved here when I was six. So, you girls have subs?"

"We do. How about you?"

"I'm just getting into this. I have this boy, a senior, and he is my sub, and he's very obedient. I've only experimented a little with dominating him. Perhaps you girls can give me some tips."

"Absolutely," Julie said. "We're old hands at this. We each have two subs, which we highly recommend. Have a seat."

Nadia was a perfect fit, a kindered spirit, but still a bit unsure of herself and her powers. Julie and Heather considered it a challenge to educate her, and turn her into a very confident dominant. The three musketeers, Heather thought. We have a group, a club.

It turns out that Nadia's seventeenth birthday was just weeks away from theirs, so the all decided to have a party and each to bring one sub. They were wondering where to hold it, and Heather suggested Steve's place in Montecito. "It's a fucking mansion, five bedrooms, plenty of room to play. Just have to find out if it's cool with Steve."

Steve was good with it if they did it at a time he wasn't using the place, so they pulled out the calendar and found a date around birthday time, when Steve was certainly going to be away.

Julie had a sedan that would seat six, so she offered to drive them all up the coast. It was agreed that they only bring subs from school, not Heather's adult sub, who might make it rather awkward. The boys wouldn't say anything about it, as that would put a target on their backs, bringing them ridicule. In fact, the boys might enjoy having friends with the same kinks, just as the girls have been enjoying their new friendship.

Nadia was getting a bit braver, and she suggested that they bring extra panties and make the boys parade around it them. "OMG," Heather said. "What a great idea." It was a done deal, and all Heather had to do was tell Lisa.

"Mom, me and a couple of my girlfriends would like to have a party to celebrate our birthdays, and Steve said we could use his place. We'll bring dates, and I promise, no alcohol or drugs."

"I was hoping to take you out for your birthday."

"Yeah, mom, that can still happen. The party will be on a day near all our birthdays, but on the real day, I'm all yours."

"I trust you when you say no drugs or alcohol. You wouldn't lie to me. I assume these dates are your subs."

"Yeah, mom. What else would we want to date."

"And I'm not going to get any angry phone calls from their mothers?"

"We won't make the boys do anything they are

unwilling to do. It going to be memorable for them and for us."

Lisa gave Heather a hug and reminded her that this was her night to make dinner. Heather, always trying to be the good daughter, got right on it, making a meat loaf, some fresh veggies and a salad.

Chapter 7

The three girls became inseparable, eating lunch together every day, hanging out after school, and being so happy with the new friendship, that they were neglecting their subs. The boys started whining about this, and the girls, not wanting to lose them, promised more time with them.

Heather's adult sub, Kirk, was very busy at work, so it wasn't a problem seeing less of her, which is why she kept him. There was no particular thrill about having an older sub. Guys were guys from puberty on. However, she was curious about this sixty year old writer, and what new stuff she might discover with him.

The birthday party was to be held a couple of weeks before her actually birthday, a week after Julie's birthday, and a month before Nadia's birthday. They decided that the girls will sit in the front seat of the car, the boys in the back. The question was whether they should tell the boys about the panty thing in advance or spring it on them at the party. Julie wanted to wait and see how they reacted, but Heather was more cautious.

"If one of them complained to his mother, Lisa would come down on me hard. She said my lifestyle wouldn't be a problem unless she got caught in the middle of it."

They agreed to tell the boys up front, and if they refused, they would be discarded, no longer subs.

This was to be a one day event, not an overnighter. Tommy's mother was very protective, and wouldn't hear of it, and quite frankly, as much as Lisa trusted Heather, there were too many things that could go wrong with six teenagers alone in a mansion in Montecito. A quick inventory of potential problems convinced Lisa. "You have the whole day, Heather.

Make good use of it, and be home before midnight."

Having Lisa fill the maternal role made Heather feel good, feel loved, feel noticed, and she said, "Yes, Mom. Before midnight to be sure."

Lisa was less worried about the girls than the boys, who were obviously under the control of the girls, and control often leads to out of control problems. She was afraid the girls would try to outdo each other with respect to dominating their boys.

Heather packed sodas and sandwiches and had the others meet her at her home. The plan was to take the coast, as it was actually faster than the 101. If they left at 8AM, they would have over 10 hours to play in Montecito before heading home, more than enough time to have all the fun they needed.

The boys, having not met before, were rather shy at the outset, but they dutifully crawled in the back seat, while the girls piled in the front, Julie driving. They passed about sodas, buckled in and off they went up the coast through Malibu and on toward Oxnard, music blaring, Julie singing with her amazing voice.

Heather had her own key to Steve's place, and Nadia was amazed that her new friend knew a famous movie star, and was something like his adopted daughter. "Will he be here today?" she asked.

"Nope," Heather responded. "He's doing some movie shoot somewhere else. But, he said we had to clean up after ourselves, or no more invitations. You boys heard that. It's your responsibility to make sure the house is like we found it."

The boys, already cowed, agreed.

The highlight of the day was the birthday show the boys had to put on for the girls. They had to put on girl's panties, and parade around like models on a runway, while the girls hooted and howled. What Heather failed to notice was that Tommy took a picture of the other boys in panties, thinking he'd tease them with it later. Show over, lunch made, eaten and cleaned up, the sun slowly sinking, the girls took their boys to various bedrooms for sexual service. Heather had no idea what Julie or Nadia would do, but she was a fan of receiving oral, and sat on Tommy's face while he serviced her. Then she told him to masturbate while she watched.

Just after nine, Heather said they had to leave, just in case of traffic or something that would make them late. Six rather tired kids had a mostly silent drive back to Santa Monica, arriving around 11:30. Heather hopped out of the car and said goodbye to her friends and found Lisa still up, sipping a glass of wine and reading a book.

Lisa was pleased with Heather's following of her rules, and stayed up chatting with her about the day. When Heather told her about the panties, Lisa said she hoped the boys wouldn't say anything to their parents, as that might not set too well.

"Mom, the boys would be too embarrassed to admit to that, so no problem."

It might not have been a problem had Tommy's mother not been so controlling. She picked up Tommy's phone and almost immediately saw the picture of the other boys in girl's panties, posing as if they were girls. That prompted an early morning call to Lisa.

"What kind of pervert do you have there. I know Thomas would never think of doing something like that himself. That had to be your Heather. I remember she got into some trouble three years ago, so I'm guessing that this was her doing."

"Excuse me, but you have to remember that these boys volunteered to go with the girls, agreed to whatever play they were involved in, and no one got hurt. What about the possibility that your boy had unprotected sex with my daughter? I don't know, but it's something I worry about. Do you think he would drop out of school to be a father if he gets her pregnant? I don't know anything about your son, but I do know about teen boys and their obsession with sex. Can you assure me that he acted responsibly? How many teen girls have had to endure an abortion while the boys suffered no repercussions? I think you should have a long talk with your boy before calling to accuse my daughter of anything." Lisa was a good prosecutor, and she knew the value of a good offence. She managed to cow this absurd woman, and get her off the phone. Then, as Heather was coming into the kitchen for coffee and breakfast, Lisa said, "Problem. Your Tommy took a picture of the boys in panties, and his mom saw it. You should not have let them take pictures."

"That sneaky little shit. I told them not to do

that, but he must have sneaked it while we were watching the others. I'll deal with him in school today."

"Quietly and low key, if you don't mind."

Heather hated being reprimanded by Lisa, and she was angry with Tommy for disobeying her orders and causing trouble. She took him aside before the start of classes.

"You are in trouble boy. Your mom called mine and complained about the picture you took. I am seriously considering ending my involvement with you, tossing you aside like the trash you seem to be. What do you think of that?"

Tommy was so deeply into his role as submissive that this threat caused him to panic. "Please, Mistresss, don't do that. I promise to be a good boy and never disobey again." He was so upset, he almost got on his knees, but Heather shook her head.

"I'm going to have to decide what to do about you, but for now, you are excused. Now go away."

Tommy slinked off, realizing how much he had learned to consider himself a submissive, and how that role had become important to him, and as he walked away, head down, Heather started thinking that maybe it was time for a new sub. However, with her birthday coming up, plans with both Lisa and with Steve, she was too busy to spend much time thinking about Tommy.

Chapter 8

Lisa knew Heather liked Italian food, so she took her to Orto Santa Monica, and since she was well known there, the waiter turned a blind eye to Heather having a glass of wine.

They had just settled in when Steve arrived and joined them. "Can't have my two favorite girls dining without me. Happy birthday Heather. You are now an official adult. How does that feel?"

"Actually, damn good dad. But since you and mom are going to pay my college tuition next fall, I don't really feel like an adult yet."

Steve said that he was happy about how the place was left, except that he found an empty beer bottle in the trash, and he was pretty sure that alcohol was not allowed.

"That was Julie. As soon as I found out she had beer, I told her no more, put the rest in the car and toss the empty. That was the only beer the whole day." She even made the gesture of crossing her heart to drive her point home.

It had been a couple of days since her birthday, and she was seriously thinking of getting rid of Tommy. She was bored with him and his whiny attitude, but she didn't want to be down to only one sub. Then her phone rang.

"Hello, Heather?"

"Yes, who is calling?"

"It's Sage, remember Sean said..."

"Yeah, I remember." She cut him off. "So are you ready to be my new sub?"

That was abrupt and took him by surprise. "Ah, well, maybe."

"Maybe doesn't do it for me. That's a yes or no question."

Sage was stunned for a moment. Wow, he

thought, right to the point, and no nonsense. Well, better to go along and see what happens. "Yes."

"I think you mean yes mistress. Isn't that right?"

Again, she was putting the squeeze on him. "Yes Mistress."

"Good boy. I think you will be easy to train. You want Mistress to train you?"

She was coming down hard, but what the hell, he'd see it through. "Yes Mistress."

"Where does my possible sub live?"

"I live in Malibu." Silence on the other end, so he added, "Mistress."

"Good boy. Any plans for Saturday afternoon?"

By now he was getting the routine. "No plans Mistress."

"Good boy. Give me your address and I'll come by around two. Will that work for you sub?"

"Yes Mistress, that will work fine."

After she hung up, Sage was feeling a mix of emotions. She really came on strong, was so absolutely sure of herself. He actually felt he had to say mistress to her. Oddly, the conversation was rather sexually exciting, but he didn't want to think about why it was. He wondered if she would be wearing leather and holding a whip or wearing high heels or any of the things usually associated with a dominatrix. But, he thought, she just turned eighteen, hardly more than a kid. How would this play out?

Sage realized he had no idea of the proper protocol for dealing with a dominatrix, so he went on line, found some sites and started to study up, research for a possible book, he thought. One common theme was that the sub was to kneel in front of the dom, and that was the case almost always. Well, he thought, a good place to start. See if that impresses her.

He was actually getting a bit nervous as two o'clock came around. He hoped she'd be on time, but she didn't arrive until 2:15. He opened the door, and she walked in, a very attractive young woman. She just stood there looking at him, not saying a word, and then he remembered and dropped to his knees. "Greetings Mistress."

"Hum, it looks like you are losing your hair sub. Oh well, other than that, you look pretty good for an old guy."

Good grief, he thought, I'm being judged like a dog in a kennel show. He didn't know how to respond, so he just said, "Thank you Mistress. I'm glad you approve."

"I'm not sure yet if I approve. Let me take a look around." She walked past him and wandered around the living area and kitchen. "Not too messy. That's a point in your favor. Now, what do you look like without your clothes?"

"I beg your pardon Mistress."

"You heard me. I want to see you naked, so strip."

He almost told her to drop dead, but he started taking off his clothes, feeling very self-conscious and vulnerable. She just stood there, stone faced, while he disrobed. He hesitated at his underwear until she pointed and motioned. He got the point and dropped them, revealing an erection he hadn't anticipated. He suddenly felt very uncomfortable, willing his cock to go down, but the more he tried, the harder he got.

She walked up to him and grabbed his cock. "Very nice. I guess you're not too old to use this." With that, she gave it a painful squeeze. "Now, I'd like a glass of wine."

He wanted to say that since he was naked, she should be also, but something in her look told him not to go there. Instead he went into the kitchen and brought out two glasses of wine. "Would Mistress like to have a seat?"

She sat down in a chair, so he couldn't sit next to her, and then she asked him to tell her about himself.

His favorite subject, so he started in about his education, his books, his hobbies and all that, while she just sat and listened attentively.

Then she got up and walked slowly around him, pausing to slap his butt. "You'll have to firm this up for me."

This was humiliating, having this girl criticize his body, treat him like an object. It was both humiliating and oddly a turn on. The idea of being a sex object was somehow very exciting, and he was getting drawn into it. "Yes Mistress, I will work on that."

"Good boy. I think you have real potential. I will mold you into the perfect sub. But first let me see you jerk off."

He was being trained, molded by this young girl, and part of him wanted to tell her to get lost, but part of him was bending to her iron will. "Yes, Mistress." Then he stood there before her, masturbating until he came, which was quickly.

"I have to go now, but I will see you next weekend. You will be available. I'm thinking of replacing another sub, and you will be his replacement. Understood?"

"Yes Mistress, understood."

"Oh yes, no orgasms without my permission, and don't you dare try to lie to me."

No orgasms? I don't think so, he thought, but he said, "Yes Mistress."

He had no idea he would feel this way, schooled, handled and left naked. She was good, and he was hooked. He could hardly wait until the next weekend.

Oddly, he actually tried to masturbate, but her words stopped him, leaving him horny and waiting for her pleasure.

Monday at school, she told Julie about Sage, and how he was very obedient. "I could tell he was just playing at first, but I think I captured him."

"You going to see him again?"

"Next weekend, and I think he'll be Tommy's replacement."

"Then give Tommy to me."

"Fine he's yours. Tell him I said so."

Tommy was fine with that. Julie actually excited him even more than Heather, and she allowed him to have sex more often.

Nadia was annoyed when she heard. "How come you didn't offer him to me? I'm the only one without a second sub."

"I'm sorry. Julie asked, and I didn't think you'd want him. Perhaps Julie will share."

"That's fine. I'm a big girl and can find my own subs."

Heather was sure she could. The girl was on the way to being a first class dominatrix, but Heather didn't want to do anything to damage this new friendship. She hadn't realized how lonely she'd been before Julie and Nadia had come into her life. She was starting to understand how a lack of friends had been making her angry and resentful. She now had loving parents and two good friends. The subs, well, she liked having them, but it wasn't the same thing. She didn't respect them, but they were fun to play with. She was pretty sure this new one hadn't been serious, but she thinks she'd broken him and will make a docile sub of him without much effort. She tried to remember when she had become so confident about males, so sure of herself around them.

Steve was finishing up his latest film, and he was planning to spend a bit of time at his Montecito place, rather than getting in the way of Lisa, who was very busy with some high profile cases. Now that Steve knew Heather had two good friends, he invited them up for a couple of days, just the girls. "Don't bring your subs. This is a chance for me to get to know your friends and just kick back."

The girls got into Heather's slightly used car, one that Lisa and Steve had got her for a graduation present, even though graduation was over a month away. They left Friday after school, drove up the coast and planned to spend the weekend with Steve. Nadia was very excited at the possibility of meeting one of her favorite movie stars. Julie wanted to know if Steve would let them have a drink or so, and Heather said he probably would, seeing that they wouldn't be driving anywhere. She let her friends know that movie people tend to be very open minded, and don't always follow the rules.

Three years of being in a domestic relationship had slightly dulled Steve's sex symbol image, a little more around the waist, a bit less hair, but he was still an impressive man, but to a sixteen year old girl, he was an old man, good looking but old just the same.

Since the girls had already spent a day there, he didn't bother to give them a tour. "I'll give you girls some wine if I don't get in trouble with your parents, okay?"

They assured them that it wouldn't be a problem, and Nadia said she wouldn't even mention it to her folks, as Sikh, they were strictly non-drinkers.

Heather realized that this was the weekend she was supposed to see Sage, but in the excitement of spending the weekend at Steve's with her friends, she'd totally forgotten. She called him and said that something had come up, and that, if he were free, she would see him the following weekend. It was obvious from the tone of his voice that he was disappointed, but it was also obvious that he was hooked and would be available.

Nadia was basically star struck, amazed that a famous movie star, one whose films she'd watched, at least his early action films, was in the kitchen getting her a glass of wine and fixing a meal. She wanted to know all about him.

It was a warm late afternoon and Julie and Heather decided to go for a swim, Steve's pool being large enough to swim laps. Nadia decided to hang around Steve and find out all about him.

"How did you get together with Lisa?"

"She was going to take me to court, but changed her mind, and fixed the problem. So, I took her to lunch, and we became friends, and it was only friends for a long time. I didn't think I was ready to settle down, but Lisa has a way about her."

"So, being married, how come you have two houses?"

"We both have very busy careers, and if we were under the same roof, we would be tripping over each other. Besides, this is too far for her to commute, and would you rather live in her place or here? We have the best of both worlds. Sometime she comes here, sometimes I go there, and sometimes we're just too damn busy to spend time with each other."

"That's not the traditional kind of thing like my parents have, but honestly, I don't think they are that happy with each other."

"Can't speak for them, but sometimes too much togetherness is more trouble than joy. Think you'll ever want to have a husband and kids?"

"Maybe, but my husband would have to know I was the boss in all things."

Steve shrugged his shoulders and looked at this young woman. "I guess there are guys out there who would be fine with that. There is every kind of relationship you can imagine out there, but some are more common and easier to find. Good luck."

Heather and Julie came in. Julie looked at Steve in the kitchen, chopping onions and it didn't fit with her image of a movie star. "Wow, the famous Steve

Longwood is making dinner for us. Makes me feel special."

Steve stopped what he was doing and asked the girls to sit down. "Just to set the record straight, you three are special indeed. You are good people, honest and decent, and I'm happy to have you in my home. Now, in my house, all guests, special or not, have to contribute, so I have kitchen chores for all of you."

After dinner, as they all lounged in front of his big screen TV, Lisa called and asked if the girls were a bother. Steve answered, loudly enough for the girls to hear, "Absolutely not. In fact they are stars in my new movie, Steve Longwood the domestic family man."

The following morning Steve promised to lead the girls up the Wiman trail to the reservoir, a short but scenic hike, a good morning walk before breakfast. Nadia was surprised how fit Steve was, hiking at a brisk pace, faster than she thought an old guy could walk.

Chapter 9

While the girls were feeling special, Sage was feeling very conflicted. He intended to play at being a sub, but this girl was good, and he was starting to think of himself as a submissive, fantasizing about serving Heather sexually and in any other way she wished. He didn't want to go there, but something about it was compelling, and he didn't know what the hell to do about it, so he called Sean.

"That girl, she's something else buddy."

"How so? You didn't let her get to you I hope."

"I think she is getting to me, and I'm not sure if I can just walk away."

"Shit, Sage, she's barely eighteen, and you are old enough for the senior discount. Get serious dude."

"come on man, you gotta feel her power, her assurance and all that."

Sean looked up from the phone, thought about his last session with Heather and finally said, "She does have that way about her, but you can't just fall into her trap or whatever it is."

"I know, I know. I'll stop it before it goes too far. Thanks buddy."

Sean made a note to discuss Sage with Heather on her next session, which was coming up the next day.

"Mister Williams, Sean, did your friend Sage tell you we met?" Heather was dressing nicer, more like she cared about her appearance, nicely fitting jeans and a sweater that showed off her good body.

"Yes, and you seemed to have made an impression. You also, I hear, have some new friends and you have changed you style of dress. Seems you may have lots to talk about."

Heather looked closely at him and waited a moment before answering. "Did Sage discuss our first meeting?" When Sean shook his head, she asked, "Do you want to hear about it."

Of course he was curious, very curious, but he was still a professional, so he turned it back on her. "If you'd like to talk about it, I'd like to hear."

A faint, knowing smile came over her, as she picked up clues in the way he worded it and the looks on his face. I think they call that voyeurism, she thought, and she wanted to watch his reactions as she told the whole story, making a point of her making Sage undress for her.

It was clear that Sean was anxious to hear the details, so she held nothing back. After several minutes describing the encounter, she asked him what he though about it.

"It sounds like he was a latent submissive, and you've brought it out in him. What now?"

"I've dumped my school sub, so maybe Sage will be my new one. Depends on how well I can train him."

For a moment Sean's imagination went to his writer friend being trained by this girl, being trained to serve her as a good, obedient sub, and it was hard to imagine. Sean remembered when the two of them had a big adventure in Arches National Park, hiking back into the wilderness, climbing rock walls. Sage wasn't the kind of guy to be trained by some young gal.

For the first time in a long time Sean wasn't sure what to ask next, so he reached for the obvious after repositioning himself to look Heather in the eye. "So, what about training your sub appeals to you?"

That seemed to take her by surprise, and her cocky look melted for a moment while she considered putting something into words that hadn't been named before.

"Well, let's see. I've always hated bossy guys, the kind who think they know better than girls, you know, the guys who only think of girls as sex objects. I guess now I sort of think of guys as sex objects and servants. I do like to be waited on, obeyed and all that. I guess I want to feel important, to feel respected. The best way to do that is to train a guy to be a good sub."

"Does being obeyed give you some sexual thrill?"

"Yeah, it really does. Making a guy undress and kneel at my feet is a total turn on."

Sean got a quick image of his friend Sage kneeling naked in front of this girl, and it was simply weird. "I assume you take the lead in sexual activities?"

"Always. I tell guys I'm going to take them in whatever way I like. I really like making them give me oral sex, sometimes while I'm drinking a soda or watching TV, like I'm almost bored while they work hard to satisfy me."

Now Sean was back grounded and knew the direction he needed to go. "So, it's as much about power as it is sex?"

Heather brightened and smiled, slightly rearranging herself in the chair. "Power, yes, power over guys is a total turn on. Sometime I don't even touch them, just watch them follow my orders. Guys need to learn that women can rule, and they can learn to follow."

"Would you ever consider an equal relationship?"

"I don't think so, but I'm young, so who knows, like when I'm old, like forty or something. I might want to settle down and marry some guy, maybe even have a kid, but who knows. Forty is a long way away."

Sean was fascinated at the honesty he was hearing. Heather wasn't holding anything back, and she was obviously proud of her power over her subs. He was reluctant to have the session end, and they hadn't even discussed the issue of the dead boys, her troubled past.

Lisa wanted a romantic weekend with Steve in Montecito, minus Heather and her friends. The question was how much latitude to give the girl, now a legal adult. "Heather, while I'm gone, you can bring one boy over, but no booze, and I don't want your friends using my bedroom. Are you good with that?"

"Absolutely, mom. You know I'll never do anything to damage your trust. If it wasn't for you, well, I have no idea where I'd be or if I'd still be alive."

Heather had already pretty much made up her mind to dump Tommy. She was tired of him and the photo thing still angered her. Kirk was out of town with his company, so she decided to invite Sage over for the weekend, hopefully to complete his training and make him a good sub. "This is Heather. Are you free next weekend?"

He had tentative plans to hike with some friends, but his curiosity about Heather and her ability to dominate him was too much of a forbidden fruit to resist, so he said he be there. He had no idea what to expect, but he figured if things get too uncomfortable, he could just leave. After all, there was no way she could hold him there against his will. At least he didn't think so.

Sage was nervous as he looked at the nice, middle class home in an upscale part of Santa Monica. Heather had said her folks would be gone, and it would just be the two of them, but as he stood on the porch, getting ready to knock, he had the urge to get back in his car and leave. Still curiosity is hard to overcome, and he wanted to see just what a dominant female could and would do with him, so he gave the door an assertive knock.

After a few moments Heather opened the door and just stared at him, making him uncomfortable, and he wasn't sure if he should ask to come in or wait for her to say something. Finally, she smiled and said, "Come in sub." I guess she considers me her sub now, he thought, and he stepped carefully into the house, a place clearly not decorated by an eighteen-year-old girl, stylish décor without being ostentatious. Heather's mom was obviously an educated professional, a woman with taste.

Heather closed the door and locked it before turning to Sage and saying, "Take off all your clothes now."

"Now? I don't know."

She unlocked the door again. "Clothes off or leave now."

She had him, so he started to slowly undress, feeling very self conscious, as she relocked the door and just stood there watching him. After his clothes were in a heap on the floor, she smiled and said, "Good boy. You respond well to training. I may decide to keep you. Now on your knees in front of me."

He knew refusal would mean the end of this meeting, so he dropped to his knees. Heather then kicked off her shoes and said, "Now kiss my feet as a sign of obedience."

That was the last thing he wanted to do, but he

found himself bending down and kissing her feet, not knowing how long she expected him to do that. "Lick my toes while you're at it. Ah yes, good boy."

There he was stark naked, kissing and licking this girl's feet, feet she hadn't bothered to wash.

"Sub, do you know how to give a girl good oral sex?"

It took him a moment to respond, but then he said yes.

"Yes, who, sub?"

"Yes Mistress."

"That's better. You will always address me as Mistress. Is that clear?

"Yes Mistress, it is clear."

"Good boy. Now I'll get undressed and find out if you really know how to please your mistress."

Slowly, casually, she started to undress, not really looking at him, seemingly thinking of something else. Sage started getting an erection, finding that it made him embarrassed. He was really in uncharted waters here.

Finally, she was totally naked, and he saw that she had a sexy body, not outrageously sexy, but sexy enough. She pulled up a chair and sat down, spreading her legs, and it was obvious what she wanted him to do, so he did his best to please this girl, his Mistress. After a few minutes, she had an orgasm. And then she asked him if he wanted to have an orgasm, and he answered, "Yes Mistress, please."

She dropped a wash cloth in front of him and said, "Now, masturbate for your mistress."

That, he felt, was tremendously hot, and within two minutes he had a powerful orgasm, better than he normally had with regular intercourse.

He looked up at her, still breathing hard, and she smiled and called him a good boy, and asked him what he had to say. He was starting to get the idea, so he said, "Thank you Mistress."

She moved over to the couch, while he was still on his knees. "You respond well to training sub. Now go into the kitchen and find the bottle of ice tea. You will bring me a glass and pour one for yourself, and hurry. Mistress is thirsty."

He quickly came back with two glasses, handed one to Heather and started to sit down next to her, but she shook her head and pointed to the floor. There he was kneeling on the floor, sipping the damn ice tea while she relaxed on the couch.

"My mom wants the house vacuumed and dusted, and I am assigning that job to you. If you do a good job, there may be another orgasm in for you, perhaps something more intimate."

This was almost too damn much. Domestic service, but he was realizing that she had him, and he couldn't refuse, so he went to work cleaning while totally naked, hoping he would be able to have sex with her after he finished.

An hour later he was done and Heather seemed satisfied. "Good boy. Now into my bedroom." She pointed to her door, and he started to anticipate what may lie ahead. She followed him in and told him to get on the bed, face up. Then she straddled him, sitting on his face. Within minutes she'd had another orgasm, and she crawled off. Then she took his cock, hard again, and started stroking it, calling him a good, obedient sub. He lost all control and simply came all over himself, almost passing out from the incredible release.

"Who do you belong to now sub?"

"I belong to you Mistress."

"And don't you ever forget it sub. Now stay where you are."

She got up and started to get dressed. Then the doorbell rang, and Heather went to answer it. Sage could hear the conversation through the open door. "Julie, hi. I'll bet you are curious to see the new sub. He's in my room. Take a look."

Sage was almost ready to panic. Who was Julie, and what did Mistress have in mind?

A tall, very attractive young woman walked in, Sage still naked on the bed, and looked him over. "So you are Heather's new sub. I hope she is training you well. I am Mistress Julie."

Not sure of how to respond, Sage just said, "Glad to meet you Mistress Julie."

"Heather, are you going to share your sub?"

"Sure. He gives very good head, and I'm sure you'll like it."

"Yeah, but I don't want you watching."

Heather left the room, closing the door behind her. Then Julie undressed, and Sage thought she had an even better body that Heather, very athletic, long well-muscled legs. He knew what he had to do and did the best he could, considering that his jaw and tongue were both tired from servicing Heather.

After her orgasm, Julie said, "Yes, Heather has a very good sub. I'm pleased."

"Thank you Mistress Julie," he said, realizing his place, coming to grips with the idea that these girls could do whatever they wished with him.

"Does the sub want to cum again?"

"I think I'm too tired. Mistress Heather had me come twice already."

Julie got dressed wordlessly and left the room, closing the door behind her. Sage wasn't sure what to do, and since he hadn't been instructed, he felt he better just wait on the bed for whatever else they had planned for him. However, after a few minutes, he was getting impatient and was about to get up when Heather came into the room with his clothes. "Sorry sub, but Julie and I have stuff to do, so you'll need to get dressed and leave." She tossed the clothes on the bed next to Sage and turned without waiting for his response. He got dressed and walked into the living room, where Heather and Julie were sitting around with cups of tea, talking. They didn't turn to look at him, so feeling foolish, he quietly let himself out, feeling like he wanted to cut the ties with these girls.

Julie watched him leave and turned back to Heather. "You were pretty cold to that sub."

"He has to learn his rights, or rather his lack of rights. I think he's starting to get it. But we don't need to bother with him right now. What are your graduation plans?"

From being a kid, a student, to becoming an adult, a graduate, is one of the major transitions in life, and this step was not wasted on the girls. They were not plugged into all the activities that make high school a rich experience, so Julie with her few friends and Heather with only two friends, had to improvise some activity to commemorate this occasion. However, they weren't sure what to do until Lisa made a suggestion. "How would you two girls like to take a cruise down to Mexico for a few days, Los Angeles to Ensenada and Cabo? Five days on me, a reward for doing really well in school."

"Damn Heather, your mom is so cool. All my mom gave me for graduation was tuition for college next year."

"Mom has lots of money, and I suspect Steve kicked in most of it. He's super rich. He doesn't advertise when he spends."

The idea of the cruise was exciting, and Julie wondered, "Even though Nadia isn't graduating, it would be fun to take her along. I wonder if that's possible."

"I'll mention it to mom. Maybe we can make it happen."

Steve was home when Heather brought it up, and he said he really enjoyed Nadia, and he'd be happy to pay her way on the cruise. "Do you girls want to share a cabin or each have her own?"

Julie was dumbfounded. "Separate cabins? Wow. That's really expensive."

"Oh, yeah. I guess I should leave some money for my kids. That's right, I don't have any kids, so I guess you three girls are as close as it comes."

Nadia's mom said yes, and what else could she say to a movie star who was going to pay the girl's way.

The three of them were hanging out on the deck, soft drinks in their hands, wearing shorts and tank tops, when some guys came up to them and started hitting on them. Julie said, "I'll take this. Okay boys, here's the deal. We are dominant females, and we are only interested in guys who call us Mistress and obey our every order. If that's not you, maybe you should walk away."

That stopped them in their tracks, and they looked at each other for some response. Finally one of them said, "Crazy bitches. You're not hot enough for us to put up with your game." Thus saving face, they walked, more like slunk away.

The girls found that it was pretty easy to get served in a bar in Cabo, so they spent the afternoon, walking, shopping and stopping for a drink before boarding the ship again.

The girls had taken some extra time off school for the cruise, but in these last weeks, there was little of importance to be missed, in face, according to Heather there was little of importance that couldn't be learned simply by reading. Teachers, she figured, were just talking heads, trying to kill the fifty minutes of class time. Even the questions from other students were pointless and boring, in her opinion.

One serious topic that came up during the cruise was college. Heather wasn't sure what she expected, but the thought of her and Julie going to different places hadn't registered. "Julie, I think my mom can get me into UC Berkeley. It's where she went to school, and she knows people."

My parents can't afford UC tuition, and they can't afford the dorms. Looks like I'll be going to Cal State, probably Dominguez Hills, because it's close, and I can commute. But Cal State Channel Islands is smaller and cute, but it's an hour away in Camarillo."

"Camarillo is not too far from Montecito. Maybe I can talk Steve into letting us stay there during the week, roommates, and I'd be happy to go to that little college."

Two eighteen years old girls on the cusp of graduation, sitting in a little bar in Cabo, looking out at the water and the iconic arch, sipping wine and planning their futures, hoping to continue this friendship as university students, they hugged and said they were ready for this.

"Monday through Friday, no one uses the master bedroom. No wild parties? Just two dedicated students going to class and studying? Is that about right?" Steve was trying hard to act the role of the serious parent.

"Absolutely, dad," Heather replied. We will attend classes, come home, take a dip in the pool, eat some of your wonderful food and study."

"And you'll replace some of that wonderful food so I have something to eat when I show up."

This time it was Julie who said. "We promise to replace anything we eat, and we'll keep the place super clean."

"If Lisa agrees, I'm okay with it. However, weekends, back to Santa Monica. Your mom will want to see you, but don't bring your laundry home. I have a washer and dryer. Also, you clean the place. Don't make some boy do it for you." With that he laughed, always considering their kinks as something amusing.

Lisa knew that other than their dominant activities, both girls were dependable, honest and trustworthy, and even though she wanted Heather to have the college experience she had, she figured it was almost going away to school. Still, it was important that she talked to Heather about this, about giving up an excellent chance at a UC education in order to hang out with her friend at a minor university.

"Sit down Heather. We need to talk." She tried to sound casual about this, but being a prosecutor, she had a way about her that had become natural, and Heather was concerned.

"Is something wrong Mom?" Heather was sitting on the end of the couch, leaning forward to show she was being attentive.

Lisa realized the impression she was giving, so she smiled to put Heather at ease. "No sweetie, nothing's wrong. I just wanted to see if you have thought through your decision about college. There is a huge difference between the UC system and the Cal State. UC gets better professors and there is the prestige thing attached to a better, need I say, more exclusive, school."

Heather interlaced her fingers and rested her chin on them, staring off into space and considering her words. "Mom, I suspect you were popular in school, at least had a bunch of friends, good parents and all that. I didn't have any of that. Julie is literally my first real friend. Nadia too. I consider you my mom, and I finally feel happy, not angry, loved, not rejected, and I can't give that up to live in a dorm with a bunch of strangers. My life is good for the first time, and I can't lose that."

"I understand sweetie. If this works for you, Steve and I are fine with it. I guess that means you'll be here on the weekends?"

"If you're not sick of having me around, yes."

Lisa reassured her that she was always welcome at home, and that actually Lisa liked the idea of having her adopted daughter around.

Steve finished the shooting on his latest film and headed to Santa Monica to see Lisa. They celebrated by going to their favorite Italian restaurant, sipping wine and catching up over some really tasty pasta.

"Are you sure you're okay with those two staying there five nights a week?"

"Not a problem. They really want this, so they'll

follow my rules. Quite frankly, it would be nice to have someone else in that big place when I get home."

   Lisa smiled at this, thinking about how Steve had changed from a playboy to an almost domesticated family man, thinking more and more about Heather as his daughter. Lisa was convinced that even the biggest playboy really wants a domestic relationship. Mostly, it's having the right woman show up, a woman who is strong and assertive and knows what she wants. Men like praise, and most would jump through verbal hoops to get it. Steve was more typical than he'd like to believe. The secret is to not tell them this, let them think they are still the dashing, hot stud that she gets all mushy over.

Chapter 10

Nadia hadn't thought about what was going to happen after her two friends graduated, but now, faced with them going away to college, she was feeling down, sad, lonely. "We'll miss you too Nadia, but remember, we'll be home every weekend, and I promise we'll get together."

The girls were getting so embroiled in their college plans that they had seriously neglected their subs, guys who were emotionally dependent on them and who assumed that not hearing from their mistresses meant that they'd done something wrong.

Kirk called Heather, almost begging. "Mistress, have I offended you? You haven't talked to me in a couple of weeks."

"My poor sub. I've been busy getting ready for college. I will come to your place tomorrow evening. You will be home."

"Of course Mistress. I'll be home all evening."

Heather was starting to realize that even as a dominant, she had obligations, expectations from needy subs, and if they weren't needy, they probably wouldn't be subs. If it wasn't for the orgasms, she would probably send her subs packing.

She decided to run her thoughts by Julie. "Do you ever get the feeling that your subs are always wanting something from you, wanting your time, wanting to serve even when you have other things to do?"

"Yeah. Once they belong to you, they want and want and whine about it."

They agreed that males are a big bother, but they are fun to play with. Perhaps, Julie suggested, that they start over when they get to college, get guys from school, so they don't have to bother with the guys back here. "After all, five days at school, but just weekends back home."

And weekends are good family days, Heather thought, family being more important than those silly subs.

Heather called Kirk, and told him she'd be over to see him that evening. He said he'd cancel his other plans, which is exactly what she expected him to do. "Have a good salad ready for me." She knew he'd go out of his way to make it good, to please her, to be a good, loyal sub.

When she arrived, she was feeling ornery and wanting to humiliate Kirk, so she ordered him to get on his knees and to kiss her feet, and since she was wearing flip flops, she just kicked them off, and Kirk dutifully got down and started kissing her feet. "Good sub. Now where is that good salad?"

He got up, dashed into the kitchen and came out with a salad as good as any in a restaurant. When he served it to her, she patted him on the head and said, "Good boy. Mistress is proud of you. I think I'll give you a reward tonight. I'll fuck you with your strapon."

He was obviously excited by this, and he said "Thank you Mistress. I would love that."

"But first, of course, you'll give me some good oral." Finishing her salad, she pushed the plate away and stripped off her shorts and panties. She sat on a chair, legs spread, and he got on his knees and buried his face in her crotch. "Ah, that's my good boy."

After she had two orgasms, she had him strip and get on his hands and knees on the bed. She, slowly teasing him, put on the strapon, cinching it up, and putting some sexual lubrication on it. All of this was done in slow motion, making Kirk get more and more excited, making him anticipate what was to come next. Then she got on her knees behind him and slowly slipped it in just a bit, teasing him, making him beg. Then she started to fuck him hard, and since he was already totally excited, it didn't take a minute or two for him to cum, gasping and moaning. He collapsed on the bed, breathing hard, unable to talk for awhile, as she removed the strapon, slapped his bare butt and got up. "I think you've had enough for one day. You are certainly my good boy. Now, listen. I'm going to start college in a few weeks, and I will only be home on weekends, and with my family and other subs, I may not have as much time for you. Do you understand?"

"Yes Mistress, but you know I'll be very disappointed."

"You have permission to find a new mistress if you'd like."

"No Mistress, I can't imagine anyone else but you."

Heather noticed that Kirk was getting hard again, and thinking it might be awhile, she ordered him to lie face up on the bed. Then she stroked his cock and balls until he was hard as a rock. Then she mounted him, moving up and down until she had a powerful orgasm. Then without a word, she got up, got dressed and said goodbye to him, leaving him on the bed, still erect. "You will need to masturbate after I leave, like the good boy you are." Obviously, she knew she didn't need to say it, seeing how turned on he is, but she knew that it was easier for him when she gave him permission.

On the way home, she imagined the same scene with that writer, Sage, and she called him when she stopped for a snack at a convenience store. "I'm looking forward to seeing you and having you. How about Thursday evening?"

Just as Kirk had said, Sage said he'd cancel his other plans. Having her sub cancel plans was a turn on for her, knowing that no matter what they had going, she was far more important, and she absolutely adored feeling that important. If only those guys three years ago were more like Kirk and Sage, they'd still be alive and maybe still serving me. It was, she rationalized, their own fault.

She went through the same routine with Sage, mostly to evaluate the difference between them. She could sense Sage's reluctance, which excited her, knowing she still had work to do on him to break his will. By the time she left, he'd lost his reluctance and was a very docile servant. She assured him that he was a good boy, and that she might not be around as much in the future, college and all that. Like Kirk, he was disappointed, but he understood and was willing to take whatever she offered. She also gave him permission to serve another mistress if he wished.

Leaving him, getting in her car and heading south toward Santa Monica, she had a vague feeling that she had made a transition, moved through another door in her life, and she realized that if she never contacted either of these men again, it really wouldn't matter one way or the other. They were just another roadside attraction on her way to who knows what. A song came on the radio, and she sang along with it, windows down, at the top of her lungs.

Sage was attempting to examine his feelings and thoughts regarding this young woman who had taken control of him. He had gotten into this relationship as a game, a way to learn about this odd lifestyle in order to understand it and perhaps write about it. He had no desire to get caught up in it, but he found, much to his confusion, that he actually wanted to obey her orders, wanted to please her, wanted to be called a good boy, a good boy forty years older than this girl. As she drove away, he realized that he could hardly wait until he could serve her again, that this submissive way of being was incredibly exciting, sexually, mentally, emotionally. She had him, and there was no way he could break the chain. In fact, there was no way he would even want to break it. Deep down he wanted to see how far she would take him down this road, wondering if there would be a point where he would refuse. The idea of a line he might not cross was a puzzle he couldn't solve, not until she took him to that line, so he was powerless at this point, and being powerless means that this girl had all the power.

Heather didn't think much about Sage once she drove away. She was focused on the future, her future as an adult, a college student, a woman with friends. She had talked to Julie about their respective majors, and Heather was going to pursue environmental science, while Julie was going to study computer science and information technology.

Chapter 11

They made plans to visit the university and decide if they wanted to attend, so one day, shortly after graduation, they jumped into Julie's car, bringing Nadia along in hopes she'd like it enough to join them the following year. The university was nestled at the base of the Santa Monica Mountains, and the girls found that there were hiking trails within blocks of the university, perfect for a cardio workout between classes. Julie had already looked at Dominguez Hills, and said she like Channel Islands better. "It's cute, and small and makes me feel like I'd be more than just a number here."

"Yeah," Heather agreed, "A place where we could be comfortable."

Nadia said she would start the process for attending the following year, agreeing that it was her kind of place. They went into the admissions office, filled out all the proper papers and was assured that there were openings in the fall if the girls were ready to commit. When asked if they needed a dorm room, Heather said that they'd be staying at her adopted father's place in Montecito, being sure to mention that dad was Steve Longwood, which impressed the admissions lady and probably made them more certain of a spot. Then they made a stop at the university cafeteria to test the food, which was quite good. As they drove away from campus, they had regarded it as a done deal, another chapter in their lives ready to be written and lived.

Unfortunately, hardly off campus streets, the girls were hit by another car, nothing serious, but a bashed in fender and broken headlight. The driver of the other car was clearly at fault, as he had run a stop sign while texting. Julie was angry that her cute little car was now damaged, and she jumped out and stormed over to the other driver, a young man wearing a university sweatshirt, obviously a student. "What the hell's the matter with you? Don't you even look where you're going?"

The guy, obviously knowing he was in the wrong and being rather intimidated by the wrath of this girl, apologized profusely, nervously pulling out his insurance information, and trying to appease her. As he was fumbling for the information, Heather got out of the car and walked up. "What's your name?"

He looked up at a face, stern but not angry, and he paused for a moment before saying, "Eddie. My name is Eddie."

"I see, Okay Eddie, you know you are responsible for getting my friend's car fixed, and at the moment it isn't safe to drive. So, what are you going to do to fix this problem?"

"Well, miss." He stopped, hoping she would say her name, but she just stood there, stern look on her face, until he managed to pull his thoughts together. "I can call my insurance company now, report the accident and get your friend a loaner and get her car to some place to get it fixed."

Heather put her hand on his shoulder. "Good boy. That's exactly what my friend would expect. Isn't that right Julie?"

Julie was calming down now that a plan had been made. "Yes, and we need it done right now, as we have to get back to Santa Monica. So, make this happen."

He was totally intimidated by these two, and he dialed his phone. When they answered, he gave all the pertinent information, adding that the girls would need a loan car right away to get them to Santa Monica. He listened for awhile and then the conversation seemed to be over.

He handed Julie the note he had scribbled. "Miss, they are sending someone to check it out and get you," He was about to say girls, but seeing how they were acting, he revised, "ladies back home." Then he remembered about contact information, wrote down his name and number hand handed it tentatively to Julie.

She looked at it, looked up at him and said, "So you are a student here?"

"Yes miss. I'm a junior. Are you students too."

"We start in the fall, at least two of us do. When we start classes, we rather expect you to make up for this by buying lunch for us and giving us a campus tour. Think you can do that?"

"Of course miss. It would be my pleasure."

"Yes, we guess it would be."

Eddie's father was quite well off and had purchased really good insurance for his son, so by the time the police had finished taking the report, a car from the insurance company drove up, and a young man, not much more than a kid, hopped out. "I've been assigned to drive you back to Santa Monica." A tow truck pulled up, hoisted Julie's car and pulled out, the driver saying that they would call when the car was ready.

The girls grabbed their stuff and hopped in with the young guy, Nadia in the front, Julie and Heather in the back. Julie looked at Heather and said, "Eddie. Are you thinking what I'm thinking?"

"If you mean, new sub, yeah, I'm thinking that he would be easy to train."

The young guy driving was straining to hear, surprised that these girls were talking about training some guy to be their sub. He had vaguely heard of this fetish, but this was the first of that kind of girl he'd ever met, and he wondered how they went about training guys. Just then Nadia put her hand on his leg and said, "You seem to be interested in their conversation. I think you might like me to train you. Isn't that so?"

His face turned red, and he stammered for a bit, trying to say he wasn't interested.

Nadia looked at him and spoke slowly in her deepest voice. "You know you want to be my loyal sub, and now you have to admit it. Come on little sub, let's hear it."

It was all the poor guy could do to drive, thinking about what this beautiful girl was saying. She was stroking his leg impatiently with her fingers, a sign that she was in a hurry for an answer. "Yes, I think I would like that."

"I think you mean, yes mistress, I would like that. Let's try that again."

By now his face was bright red and he was stuttering. "Yea, yea yes miss, mistress, I would like that."

"Good boy. Make sure I have your number and

address. I hope you have your own place."

"I, I, I live in my parents basement, separate door from outside. They don't, I mean they leave me alone, so you can, well, you know."

She was enjoying this. "So I know what exactly?"

"When you come, my parents won't even know you are there."

"My name is Mistress Nadia. Remember to always call me Mistress. Do you understand?"

"Yes Mistress Nadia. I understand."

She turned around to her friends in the back seat. "I guess you'll be coming back here before summer ends."

"Sure, got to pick up my car and pick classes and all that stuff."

"Then I'll come along and have fun with my new boy here."

"The boy, who was almost two years older than Nadia, was trying to process what had just happened. He had been given the job of taking these girls home, and now he was this cute girl's boy, to be used, he guessed, for her pleasure. He was both afraid of where this was going and also very sexually excited. He had a series of fantasies speeding through his mind, images of what she might or might not decided to do with him. He wanted to ask, but was too shy to bring it up.

As they road along Highway One, headed toward Malibu, Nadia reached over, put her hand between his legs and squeezed gently, driving the boy wild with excitement. Then she stopped. "That's enough for now. I want your full attention on your driving. We'll continue this next time."

"Yes Mistress Nadia." He was definitely hers now, and although barely seventeen, she already realized how many guys had deep fantasies they normally didn't admit, even to themselves. Here was a true submissive, one who probably didn't consider himself to be one, at least not until this moment. The power was intoxicating and very sexually exciting.

When Lisa saw the girls getting out of the insurance company's car, she had a maternal moment, a momma bear's concern over her cub, even though Heather wasn't her child, and that she was a legal adult. One doesn't change a relationship just because of another birthday. "What happened? Are you girls alright?"

Heather wanted to reassure Lisa, but also felt so good that her "mom" was so concerned. In every respect, other than biological, Lisa was her mom, and the best mom a girl could ever have.

"Mom, the car looks worse than it is. The insurance company will have it fixed in about a week. I'm to pick up a loaner at this address." She showed Lisa the piece of paper, and assured her that it was the other guy's fault.

Lisa, feeling very maternal, wanted to do something for the girls, so she suggested that Heather and Julie, along with Julie's mother, go shopping for new outfits for college, something more adult. Lisa had yet to meet Heather's mother, so she was curious. The girls loved the idea of new clothes for college, as anyone would, so a plan was made.

Julie was a tall girl, five foot ten, and, while not at all fat, wasn't not a slim young woman. Lisa had no idea what to expect of Julie's mother, Ann, but she was surprised when they met. Ann was six foot and husky, apparently raised on a ranch and had spent her teen years handling bales of hay. She was a big and strong woman with a most sweet and unassuming manner. She thanked Lisa for including her on this shopping trip, adding, "My husband is between jobs, so money is short at the moment."

Lisa assured her that whatever Ann couldn't cover, Lisa could easily. "I earn good money, but my husband is a wealthy actor with more than he can spend."

Heather hadn't met Julie's dad yet, so she asked about him. "He's a sweet man, but there is a real disconnect between my parents."

"How so?"

"You see how big mom is. Dad is five foot eight and slender. The two look odd together."

A sudden realization hit Heather, a new way of looking at the sexes. "Where is it written that a man has to be bigger than a woman? What would have happened if your mom held out for some guy taller than six foot and bigger built? You got two parents who love each other and love you, and if you had a different dad, how might that have been?"

"Yeah, a hear you. I love my dad, but sometime I'm embarrassed that I tower over him. I mean, he's a strong, positive man, but he's short, and some of the kids made fun of him."

"Does your mom dominate him?"

"I don't think so. It seem they have an almost equal relationship, but she earns more money, so she makes more financial decisions and all that. I suspect she also leads in bed."

"That sound like a female led relationship, but not domination, which is cool. Did you ever wonder how you got into being a dominant?"

"You know, I've never thought about it from that angle. I always thought I was better than boys, and I should be in charge, but I don't know why I feel that way."

Heather decided to dig up her uncomfortable past for her friend, as they walked down to the beach, out on the pier, to watch the sunset. "I never respected my dad for being so fucking passive. And I hated my mom for being such a slut. But I'm starting to see that her being a slut might have been due to the shitty relationship they had. My dad was a cold fish, and I vowed to never be in a relationship where I'm not respected and appreciated."

"Don't forget worshipped." Julie laughed at that, and Heather, seeing the irony, laughed too.

Walking around the store, the girls shopping, looking at everything, trying to decide, the moms, carefully behind, chatted. Lisa wasn't a small women, at five foot eight, but was dwarfed by Ann. "So Ann, what convinced you that your husband was a keeper?"

"I have to say, sense of humor and kindness. I've never heard him criticize another person, or have any problems with them. He is a rare man, devoid of anger."

"Steve is becoming one of those, but it's been a slow process."

The two women laughed at that. Then Ann added, blushing as she said it, "Size of cock is not related to size of the man, and Tom is well endowed."

"Isn't it wonderful," Lisa added, "that we modern woman can say what we expect sexually. Our grandmothers had few expectations sexually, and most men I guess only considered their own orgasm. We are truly liberated."

"And our daughters have taken it to a new level. How do you feel about that, Lisa?"

"Two minds, Ann. I'm not totally comfortable with the dominant thing, but I guess the guys are into it and like being used by our girls. I do know that a very angry, violent young girl is now kind and considerate, and if being a dominant is what it took, I'm fine with that."

"I get that. Julie never really fit the traditional female model, and this is how she expresses herself. It works. You know, because of the difference in size, many people think I'm some kind of dominant woman, but frankly, I'm only slightly dominant. We're mostly equal, except when there is something heavy to lift?" with that last comment, she laughed.

Julie held up a lovely outfit. "Mom, I think I'd like this."

"Let's look at the price tag first." Ann was obviously trying to watch her money.

"Ann, please let me get this. Your daughter has really transformed Heather with her friendship, and I'd like to show my appreciation."

Ann was uncertain, saying she didn't need charity, but Lisa said, "I'm walking around with a pocket full of my husband's money, and he begged me to spend it all, so I don't want to disappoint him."

Ann laughed again, a big, booming laugh, before agreeing to accept Lisa's help.

With shopping done, and bags of new outfits for the girl's first semester, they retired to a place for lunch.

They went to a place where Lisa was well known, and the owner, knowing Lisa was the prosecutor, didn't question her when she ordered a bottle of wine for the table, glasses for all four, but not before asking Ann if it was alright to let Julie have a glass.

"Don't have a problem with that. I consider her an adult now, so if she wants a drink, but not too damn many, I'm fine with that."

As they sipped their wine, ate and talked, Heather started to step back mentally and observe, seeing that this was more than just two moms and two daughters, but more like four adult friends, laughing, talking, eating and sharing their lives. This made her feel so good, so much like she belonged, that she was a part of a group of good, smart women, and she also felt loved, an emotion she still couldn't get enough of. Lisa was both mom and friend, and Ann was becoming a friend, Julie being her best friend. She was realizing that close connections like this were common among women, but much less so among men. Her impression was that so many men were emotionally lonely, and perhaps that's why they took so well to being dominated. Oddly, it seemed to make them feel wanted.

Half way through her second glass of wine, Ann had to ask the question that was on her mind. "What is it about being doms that you enjoy so much?"

The two girls looked at each other, searching on clues to how to respond. Finally Julie said, "It's mostly about the power, having power over men, making them obey our orders. Do you agree Heather?" When Heather nodded yes, Julie continued. "It seems that either guys want you passive or they are willing to be subs, and having that control, that power is very sexually exciting. I like knowing it is all about my pleasure, not some dumb guy getting off without regards to my needs."

Heather had an idea forming in her mind. "Perhaps if guys were more sensitive to female needs, we wouldn't need to be doms. Still, I love it, so maybe that wouldn't help."

"Yeah," Julie said. "I love to sit there and have them anxious to serve me. Power is awesome."

"And, these guys seem to love being dominated. They sometimes beg to be able to serve." Heather added.

Ann was about to say, since the wine was relaxing her, that occasionally She and her husband roll play, sometimes she dominates. She really likes spanking him, but looking at the others, knowing her daughter, she decided to keep it to herself.

Lisa's relationship was totally vanilla. She and Steve had a great sex life, but there were no spankings, bondage, any of that sort of thing, and she was wondering if Steve would even enjoy roll playing. After all, he'd been quite the playboy, and in all his sexual adventures, perhaps he'd experimented. She vowed to herself to bring it up one night.

A person's sexuality can be confusing, as there

are many ways to be sexual, and some seem remote or forbidden until something happens to place these options in front of one. At that point, a person's biases come up against one's sexual curiosity. For some, that means the road not taken, but for others it opens new doors, and one doesn't know what he or she will do until faced with those choices. Sage had started this as a game, a sexual diversion, something that could be written about, but he was surprised to find himself caught. Heather had touched something in him he had apparently suppressed, and now he was unable to stop thinking about her, about an eighteen-year-old girl who had dominated him and had given him one of his most powerful sexual experiences. Now, he wanted more, and now he couldn't help thinking about her as mistress. He wanted to be naked, on his knees, doing her bidding, begging to serve her. But now, she seemed to have drifted away, and he wanted her to contact him, to make him do things that satisfied his sexual fantasies. He was feeling the draw of being a submissive, and it was both humiliating and exciting, and he wanted more.

Chapter 12

Heather was preoccupied with starting the university, enjoying her new friendships and getting the feeling of being an adult, a woman rather than just a girl. She had learned to regard males as slightly more than toys, creatures to play with for fun and sexual release. She had trained herself not to take any of them seriously, to avoid any situation where she might get too involved, too vulnerable. One thing she would never be is vulnerable, which to her was another word for weak and needy. As long as she could call the shots, she was secure, comfortable, protected. She had no tolerance for women who were weak, who were controlled by men, and she felt it was either control or be controlled. She couldn't fathom anything in between, even though Lisa and Steve seemed to have a balanced relationship. They were the exception, but deep inside, she felt that Lisa was the one in charge, that Steve was so much in love with her that he would do whatever she asked, which was only a slight exaggeration. What she didn't understand was that Steve had finally found the relationship he needed but had not realized until he met Lisa. She had saved him emotionally, and he adored her for that. Heather's problem was that men seemed two dimensional to her, either men who submitted or men she totally ignored. To Heather, it didn't matter if the man was sixteen or sixty. They were all the same to her. Occasionally she thought about contacting Sage, but life was getting in the way. She had what she wanted, but she was not willing to entertain love, love being a weakness.

It took a couple of glasses of wine for Lisa to get up the courage to mention it, but there in bed, cuddling with Steve, she asked him what he thought about the whole domination/submission thing that Heather practiced, if there was any appeal to that lifestyle.

"Academic interest or something more personal?"

"I don't know, Steve. Just wondering what the draw is and if you wonder also."

Steve said that he'd done some small role play things in the past, and that it could be fun, but that it isn't a lifestyle he wanted as a default in a relationship. Lisa agreed, than asked him if he were to play, which role would he like.

He thought about it for a bit before saying "It might be fun to try it both ways."

"Yeah," Lisa agreed. "Just for fun, a game, nothing like a serious BDSM thing."

"A bit of occasional spice in the relationship?" Steve asked.

"Exactly," Lisa responded.

They agreed to set a night to experiment. Each of them would take turns in the dominant role, and each would be honest about how they felt about each scenario.

A night of experimentation failed to make converts of them, but they did make some discoveries. The strapon they bought was a bit of a hit, as they both enjoyed Lisa pegging Steve, and they decided to keep that in their play schedule, but most of the rest of the activities didn't impress them very much. Lisa said, "Well, we did get a new kink out of this, and it was fun."

"Not nearly what Heather would get excited about, I"m sure," Steve added.

Heather wasn't really thinking much about Sage, but sitting in her room one evening, she picked up the book he had given her and with little to do at the moment, she opened it up to a random page and started reading.

"And in the next instant, as I started to move away, the moment, like the shining face of creation, shattered. The flow of natural time resumed, and everything shifted slightly, consigning the moment to the imperfect past. But in that instant, the clocks, counters and odometers of life had reset once again, the old definitions had been replaced, and as I walked on, it all began again."

Heather was struck by this, by the notion that life can be reset, that the past can be tossed aside, that things can begin anew. There was much to consider in these words, and Heather was spellbound, considering the implications for her own life. One question she asked herself was if she was wedded to her past, that the course of her life was set and unchangeable. What if, as Sage had apparently done, she could just hit a reset button and become whatever and whoever she wished. Did she love her life? Did she want more? This was something she would have to think long and hard about. Her road, which had seemed fairly straight, now was seen as roads that diverge, that can be chosen, tried, abandoned if not satisfying, with new roads to select. The question that kept oozing up was something like, what do I really want out of life? If she could answer that, perhaps she would be happy.

She was realizing that having a real family and two good friends was a close to happiness as she'd ever been or even imagined, but what if there was more. She still had a gnawing feeling of being incomplete, of being very close to grabbing the brass ring, but still somehow missing it by mere inches. Something was wrong on a very subtle level, something not obvious enough to hit her between the eyes. Dominating guys had been fun and sexually rewarding, but emotionally empty. Even college, which should be an exciting lifestyle just seemed like another diversion, another chapter in a life slightly off kilter.

It was time to pick up Julie's car in Camarillo, so she drove Julie and Nadia. In the loan car the three girls rolled up Highway One past Malibu and her new sub Sage and on to Ventura County. Nadia had contacted her new boy, and it was obvious that he was adjusting his schedule to accommodate her. They dropped her at his place, telling her they'd be back late that afternoon, but if she needed them, she should call.

"By the way, Nadia, what's your boy's name?"

"Wow. I don't even know, but perhaps it's better I don't know. I'll just call him sub, and he'll call me Mistress, and that's good enough. After all, I don't think I'll be coming up here very often after you two start college. I have school during the week, and you two will be back south on the weekends. I'll enjoy the boy and then cut him loose."

The boy had been thinking about this encounter ever since he'd driven them home, and the more he thought, the wilder the scenarios had become, and he had gotten so excited at all the imagined possibilities that he could hardly contain himself, and he had a raging erection as he answered the door. "Please come in Mistress Nadia."

She walked in to his basement apartment, looked around and said, "Why are you still dressed? Don't you know you need to be naked for my inspection?"

He apologized profusely for his oversight as he quickly, nervously, removed his clothes, letting them drop on the floor. Soon he was naked, his erection testimony to the effect she had on him, and she was totally enjoying it, taking her time inspecting him, walking around him as he stood awkwardly in the middle of the room. "You are a good boy, and you've passed inspection." She sat down on the edge of the bed and kicked off her shoes. "You must demonstrate your submission before we continue. Do you know how to do that?"

"Na, na no Mistress. What do I do?"

"You must kiss my feet to show your submission, and you need to do that now."

He dropped to his knees and started kissing her feet, so excited by this demonstration of her power that he could hardly believe what he was doing, that he was totally under the control of this girl, and that her control was the most exciting thing he'd ever experienced.

"I just want to inform you, boy, that you may not cum until I give you permission. Do you understand?"

"I'll try Mistress."

"Not try, but do as you are told. Tell me you understand."

"Yes Mistress, I understand."

"Good boy. Now help me out of my clothes."

She stood there while he carefully, nervously removed her clothing, getting more and more excited with every bit of skin she exposed. Then she sat back down on the bed and said, "Do you know how to give oral sex?"

"I think so, Mistress. I've not really, you know, done it really."

"I will instruct you." She pushed his head between her legs and moved his tongue to her clit, telling him to lick and suck, and he was a quick study, trying his best to please her, to give her an orgasm so that she would allow him to have one. This girl, younger, still in high school, was so much more mature and sophisticated that he felt like a twelve-year-old on a first date.

Within a few minutes Nadia had a powerful orgasm, finally pushing his head away. "Now, stay where you are and masturbate for me. I want to see you cum like a good little horny boy."

It only took moments before he exploded, gasping and almost passing out from the excitement. Finally he looked up at her with a questioning look on his face.

"I approve boy. Now, since you've done so well, I have a special treat for you. She opened the bag she'd brought in and pulled out a strapon. It took a moment for him to realize what was going to happen, and he was somewhat afraid, somewhat concerned that it wasn't something a guy should like. "Are you sure, Mistress?"

"Don't ever question me boy. I know what's best, and I promise you will love this." She strapped it on, ordering him on the bed on his hands and knees, and then she rubbed some sexual lube on the dildo and slowly inserted it in is rear end. At first it was kind of painful, but soon he found it exciting. "Now I'm going to fuck you hard, and I'll make you cum again."

She was a girl of her word, and soon the pounding was getting him excited, as she pulled on his hips with every thrust, and within minutes he had another orgasm, finally collapsing on the bed. Without thinking of what he was going to say, he mumbled, "I belong to you my Mistress."

"I know you do. You are a good boy. Tell me what are you?"

"I'm a good boy Mistress."

She patted him on the ass and said, "Yes, you are my good boy."

She dressed, picked up her phone and left a text for her friends: "All done here, and I'm ready whenever you are." Then she told him to bring her some soda and snacks, while she turned on his TV to watch some old movie, as he sat down by her feet, still naked because she wouldn't let him get dressed.

Heather and Julie were too busy to check their text messages. They were trying to decide what to do with the guy who had hit their car. "We could enjoy him together" Julie ventured.

Heather thought a moment, got an image in her mind and frowned. "You and I on the bed with him, naked. That kind of creeps me out. There is something kind of lesbianism about it. Why don't you play with him while I grab some lunch?"

"If you're sure. I'll call and see if he's ready for company."

Heather dropped Julie off and said she'd be back in about an hour. Then she found a diner, sat at the counter and ordered a burger and coffee. What's wrong with me, she thought. I should have been anxious to play with that guy, but somehow I just couldn't get excited about it. Maybe there's no longer any challenge getting guys to submit. It's starting to become routine. I'm only eighteen, she thought, I can't be this jaded. However, she was curious about Julie and gave her a call.

"Hope I'm not disturbing your fun."

"Not really. The boy is giving me a foot message, and I'm enjoying a glass of wine. What's up girlfriend?"

"You know, maybe I should have come with you."

"Not too late. I've enjoyed him, and you can have your turn."

"Sure, I think I'd like that. Be right over."

Julie looked down at her new sub and said, "You remember Heather. Well, she would like to play with you, and I'm sure you wouldn't mind, so she's coming over."

Julie had already trained him, so he looked up and said, "As you wish Mistress." The idea of being dominated by both girls was a huge turn on, and he was looking forward to it, to getting so excited he would be out of control. Julie had made him strip, kiss her feet, give her head and get pegged for the first time, and it was an experience he never dreamed he would not only like, but crave. He was ready to do whatever these hot girls demanded of him.

Heather made him get on his knees and kiss her feet, the standard opening gesture to show obedience. Then she demanded oral and then pegged him until he came and collapsed from the excitement. Julie was waiting in the living room, and when Heather was finished with him, the two girls called Nadia and said they'd pick her up.

The three girls laughed about the boys they'd played with, as they drove home, stopping in Malibu for a snack and drinks, which they enjoyed as they watched the surfers riding the perfect Malibu waves.

"Some of these surfers are pretty cute." Nadia said after watching for awhile.

"Yeah," Julie added, "but I'll bet most of them are so into surfing, they probably wouldn't be much fun."

Heather was kind of zoning out as she watched them, noticing a few of them glanced their way as they headed into or out of the water. "Some day I'd like to find a guy who is totally not into being dominated and work on him until I break him to the saddle."

"Horse metaphor, I see" Julie giggled. "I think there are many of them that can't be broken. In fact some of them might become a problem. They might want to tame you."

"All the better. I love a challenge."

Then Julie thought for a bit. "What about that nerdy therapist you've been seeing? How about turning him into your submissive?"

"That would be a challenge because of the patient and therapist relationship. I do sense some weakness plus a lot of curiosity about the lifestyle. How about bending him over his desk and taking a strapon to him. Now that sounds like fun."

"But you have to make him beg for it."

Heather used a male voice. "Please fuck my sorry ass mistress."

They laughed, and as they did, a handsome surfer walked by, turned, smiled and said, "Good afternoon girls." But before they could respond, he walked on, launching into the surf.

"Surf is number one for that guy. Girls when there's no waves."

They all laughed, knowing that for many guys, this lifestyle would leave them cold, but they also knew that underneath many so-called alpha males, there was this urge to submit to a woman with the personal power to control them. Heather wasn't thinking that deeply at the moment, but she was formulating an exciting plan. Rather than trying to work on therapist

Williams slowly, she would just come straight to the point and see how he reacts. A test of wills, and that seemed like it could be fun.

"I'm sorry I haven't been in lately, doctor, Sean, but I've been back and forth to Camarillo, getting ready to start college and all that stuff."

"Camarillo, that little Cal State campus?"

"Yeah, you know it?"

"Yes, my daughter goes there, or I think she still does. Haven't talked to her in months."

Heather wanted to get to the point. "Okak, sure. How about an apointment this week?"

"Sure, I can get you in tomorrow afternoon, say around 3:30?"

"Perfect, I'll see you then."

Heather went over in her mind what she would say, and how she would position herself for maximum impact. This, she thought, one way or the other, would be delicious fun.

As soon as she sat down, Williams asked her what was on her mind, what was bothering her.

"It's you doctor."

"I don't understand. Me?"

She decided to bring in a bit of drama. "I've been wrestling with this lately, but I might as well get to the point, if that's okay."

"Of course, Heather. Come right out with it, that's the best way."

That's what she wanted to hear, so she leaned over toward him, as if to share a dark secret, her shirt open, showing some cleavage. "I've decided to make you my new submissive, my sex slave, my pet."

A rush of emotions surged through his mind, and it took what seemed a very long time to sort it out and come back with an answer. This was shocking, and off-putting, but in some way rather exciting in a strictly forbidden way. While he tried to formulate his thoughts, she just sat there, leaning forward, smiling, not moving a muscle.

"That was, that was quite abrupt, and I'm not sure how to respond other than saying thank you but no thanks. I can't have that kind of relationship, not with you, not with a patient, not with anyone."

Without a moment's hesitation, she answered, "I'm going to ignore your protests. All my subs protest at first before giving in and obeying me. I've made up my mind, and that's all there is to it. However, I'll give you some time to get used to the idea. Now, I want you to go home tonight, think about this and masturbate for me like a good boy."

He started to protest, but she held up her hand. "Don't say anything. You have your instructions, and I know you will follow them to the letter. Now, as for my issues, I think I'm over my guilt, at least on the surface. Maybe something subconscious, or who knows. We can discuss that another time sub."

She got up to leave, smiled at him and said, "It's been fun. I'll see you later good boy." And before he could respond, she was out the door, leaving him totally confused and not sure what was happening. He knew one thing for sure; he was not going to be her submissive. However, her words and massive self-confidence played on his mind, and after dinner, alone in his house, thinking about her, he was getting excited, unbidden fantasies intruding on his mind, and the more he tried to put it aside, the more excited he got until he masturbated, thinking that it would put an end to this foolishness.

He didn't realize that he was playing right into her hands, but he started looking forward to their next appointment, whenever that might be.

Heather had just a few weeks before starting school, so if she wanted this therapist as her sub, she had to act fairly quickly, but not too quickly, as she needed him to become anxious to see her. She was young, but she'd learned about the male mind, at least enough to know what they were like sexually. Men get confident and controlling when woman seems weak and easy to manipulate, but a strong woman brings out the insecure little boy in them. So, she waited a week before calling for an appointment, knowing that he would find room in his schedule for her.

She decided to get straight to the point. "How is my loyal sub Sean today? Have you missed your mistress?"

"Heather, I'm not your loyal sub, and you should call me Doctor Williams."

It was perfect. He was seated, and she was still standing, so she walked over to him and stood over him, fists on her hips, giving him a hard look for at least a minute while he became noticeably uncomfortable. Then she reached out and patted him on the head. "How cute. My loyal sub Sean is trying to be a big boy and trying to avoid calling me Mistress. It's cute, but I'll have no more of that. You must learn your place and learn to be a good boy. Look at me. You know you want to be a good boy, right Sean?"

He totally didn't expect this, and she was making him very uncomfortable. "I don't think we should go there. This isn't an appropriate topic of conversation."

"Did you forget to call me Mistress. I must insist on that, so let's start over. My sub needs to be trained. Now speak to me with the proper respect."

"Look, I don't like where this is going."

"I'm not going to have a conversation with someone disrespectful. Now address me by my proper title right now sub." Her voice was hard and cold with just a touch of anger, accompanied by a mean frown.

Sean thought he'd be able to get through to her by giving her the respect she demanded, so reluctantly he said "Mistress."

"Now you are being a good boy sub. Now what is on your mind?"

He was getting flustered. "Well, ah, you scheduled this appointment." Then he hesitated for a moment before adding "Mistress."

"Yes sub, I did, and do you want to know why?"

"Yes Mistress." Mistress came a bit easier this time.

"I'm here to train my new sub. You can't serve me unless you are properly trained, and I know you need lots of training. Now tell me you want me to train you, and don't waste my time."

There is a point in the battle of wills when one person breaks and has to give in, and Sean was just about at that point, needing only one more shove. "Now sub, before I get angry with you."

"Yes Mistress."

"Yes Mistress what? Don't make me guess."

He folded like a delicate stack of cards, her firm, demanding tone more than he could resist. "Yes Mistress, I want you to train me."

"Excellent. You want to be a good little sub, don't you?"

He had gone over the line, and he was her's now, and he knew he couldn't go back, that all he could do is completely surrender, and somehow total surrender was so inviting, like sleep after a hard day, like a warm bath. She had him, and now he wanted nothing more than to please his new Mistress.

"Yes Mistress, I want to be a good little sub."

"You will give me your address and phone number, and I will come to you and do things you've only dreamed of."

After she left, he seemed to wake from a dream. Why, he thought, did he surrender to this girl. This isn't who he was, but there was something about her that seemed to take hold of him, and he was sorry she had his number and address. He knew that she could control him with little effort if he were in the same room with her, and he hoped he could avoid that, hoped but still thinking about the thrill of what she might do with him.

He called his friend Sage, knowing he'd had some experiences with Heather. "It's Sean. I have a question about Heather."

"I haven't seen her for a few weeks. What question?"

Sean wasn't sure how to approach this with his friend. "She, well, sort of started with me in my office today, getting me to call her Mistress. I'm not sure now what to do about that."

"You are in for a wild ride, my friend. I never thought I'd be interested in being a submissive, but she certainly convinced me. Has she, well, done anything with you yet?"

"Not yet, but she has my home phone and address, and I guess she'll be coming to my place. Frankly, I'm a bit anxious about that."

Sage laughed. "Yeah, I was too, but it was really exciting, and the more I surrendered, the more exciting it was. Surrender to her. She will make it worth your while."

Sean was just a bit less anxious after the conversation, but he still had no idea why he folded when she demanded he surrender. It was, he thought, the power of her personality, the attitude that she could get whomever she wished, whenever she wished, and there was something about that he simply couldn't resist.

Yes, resistance. She literally crushed his resistance, and he was like a deer in the headlights with her staring at him over his desk, looking at him as if he were already hers to do what she pleased with.

With a mixture of dread and anticipation, Sean waited to hear from her, his fantasies running rampant. When she finally called, he wasn't exactly sure how to respond. "Hi sub. Are you ready to be mine and to experience things you've been fantasizing about?"

"Yes, I guess."

"No, no, you can't guess, and remember to address me as Mistress. Now let's hear your response again."

"Yes Mistress. I'm ready."

"Good boy. I'll come over this evening. You will be naked when I arrive, so I can inspect my new sub."

The idea was giving him an erection. "Yes Mistress, as you wish."

Sean straightened up his condo, carefully stacking the magazines he had tossed on all the tables, picked up the dishes in the living room and took them to the kitchen. Then he looked around and thought how bare the place looked. There had been more art on the walls, more decorative items about when his wife had lived with him. Now, the place reflected a man who didn't care much about his home, and he was afraid Heather would react negatively to this boring place, making him look boring, and that just fed his insecurity.

When Heather told Julie and Nadia about her potential new sub, they thought it was funny. "That nerdy therapist? What are your plans for him?"

Heather had been thinking about this, knowing that very soon she would be a busy college student, so this would be short lived. "I want to try humiliation. There's been some You Tube videos, and it sounds like fun."

Julie knew about humiliation, but Nadia was confused. "How are you going to humiliate the guy Heather?"

"Not sure yet. Maybe make fun of his body or his cock if it's small. I guess I'll play it by ear when I get there. New sub, new kink."

She told them that he was to be naked when she arrived, and they thought that was a good idea. Then

Heather said, "I'm not going to say a word, like for five minutes, just walk around looking closely at him while he stands there feeling like a prize pig at market."

Nadia laughed. "You are going to crush the poor guy's ego."

"If he's insecure enough to let me do that, he deserves it. Maybe a good lesson for the future. You know, it's really hard to have any respect for guys."

Heather had been clear, seven in the evening, so Sean was ready a few minutes early. He stood naked and nervous by the front door, alternately getting erect and going soft, not sure how she expected to find him. Absurd, he thought. She's just a girl, a patient, barely an adult. How can I be so nervous about this?

Then the doorbell, and he quickly opened the door to find Heather in tight shorts and a vee neck tee shirt, looking sexy, but not obvious. Without saying a word, she walked in and stared at him, looking up and down as if evaluating some piece of merchandise. He wanted to say something, to ask something, but he was unsure and feeling awkward, painfully aware of his body and that it wasn't that of a sexy young man. It seemed like forever, waiting for her to say something, but instead she just walked around him slowly. Slapping his ass as she slowly inspected him. Then she reached down and grabbed his cock and said, "What the hell is this supposed to be?"

"It's my, my penis Mistress. Is something wrong?"

"It's so tiny. Is this the best you can do? My god, you are pitiful."

He was shocked and embarrassed. "I'm average Mistress."

She laughed loudly for effect. "And how do you know you are average? Do you and your friends compare your little cocks. Do you masturbate for each other to enjoy."

"I've read about it Mistress, I'm in the average range."

"Oh, yes, read about it in articles by other tiny cock guys, trying to make themselves and guys like you feel good about your shortcomings." She grabbed it, giving it a painful squeeze. "I've seen many of these, and you are the smallest I've ever had the disappointment to see. It doesn't even stick out as far as your plump belly. You look like the Pillsbury Dough Boy. I think you should be on your knees apologizing for wasting my time."

Every insecurity Sean had ever felt welled up in him, and he was on the verge of tears. Without a second thought, he dropped to his knees and said, "I'm so sorry Mistress. I know I don't deserve your attention."

She kicked off her shoes, put her hands on her hips and looked down at him with a scowl on her face. "What are you going to do to make it up to me?"

He looked up at her, then looked away, looked at her bare feet right in front of him and reacted almost by instinct, he bent over and kissed her feet.

"They got sweaty in these shoes and need to be licked clean you worthless sub."

He immediately started to lick her feet, surrendering to her completely, knowing she was in absolute control, knowing and giving in to his position beneath her.

She stood there for several minutes while he served her, licking her feet and realizing that he now belonged to her, that whatever she ordered, he would do to please her in any way he could.

"I'm sure you can't fuck with that little thing, but tell me, do you know how to give oral?"

"Yes Mistress, or I think so Mistress. Do you want me to give you oral sex now?"

"Yes sub. I want you to lie down on the bed, and I will sit on your face. Perhaps you can be useful after all." She reached into the bag she was carrying and pulled out a large strapon. "If you do a good job, I may use this on you."

He gave her an orgasm and then got on his knees. She lubed up the dildo and started fucking him hard, and while it hurt at first, he soon got used to it and started getting excited, finally having a powerful orgasm, collapsing on the bed, gasping for air.

"You did a fairly good job sub, but I'm going to have to spank you to keep you on your toes." She spanked his naked ass, which got him excited again. He thought he was almost ready to have another orgasm, but then she stopped, got up and started getting dressed.

"You might be worth keeping with the right

training. Are you open to being trained?"

"Yes Mistress. Please train me."

"Good boy. Don't get up. I'll see myself out."

He heard the door close, but he still didn't get up, but just lay there sprawled, wondering about his conflicted feelings, both humiliated and excited over what had just happened to him. He was going to have to confront this situation, this feeling like a submissive man who will let this young girl do what she will with him. I shouldn't let this happen to me, he thought, but below that thought was this new, taboo excitement.

At dinner that night, Heather decided not to tell Lisa about her new sub, feeling that it would seem she was throwing away her therapy. As much as she hated keeping anything from "mom," this might be a bit too much. Fortunately, Lisa was excited about Heather starting college, and she had advice and questions, and she wanted to know if Heather had decided on a major. Heather said she was still leaning toward environmental science, but she figured she had a year or two before a final decision.

"Remember, anything science requires at least a masters, probably a doctorate. That means years of school."

"Years where I can still be your little girl on weekends?"

Lisa loved that Heather wanted to stay her little girl, even though she was now a grown woman, a very strong and independent woman. "You'll always be my little girl."

Heather never tired of being reassured. In so many other ways she was totally independent, but in her relationship with Lisa, she was desperate to be the daughter, mother's little girl. It made her feel anchored, cared for, loved, and although she never thought in those terms, being loved was what she craved.

Having a cup of coffee with Julie, planning the upcoming move to college, Heather recounted, at Julie's insistence, her encounter with Sean Williams.

"Total humiliation, great. I've got to start doing that. By the way, about our little fender bender guy, are we going to keep sharing him or do you want him?"

"No, I really don't. You keep him for yourself."

"Are you sure. I mean, if you want..."

"Seriously, Julie, I have no interest in the guy. In fact, I'm having more and more trouble getting excited about these subs. You know, it's just too easy, like with this little therapist. I broke him completely in just minutes. I was hoping he'd resist, be a little rebellious, try to say no, but he just gave in completely, taking all the fun out of it."

"Maybe you need an alpha male, one you will have to spend some time taming."

"Yeah, but I don't know how to find one. It's like the submissive guys are drawn to me like bees to honey. The others, well, they don't seem to pay much attention to me."

"I guess you'll have to work harder if you want one. Look at that guy over there."

"The guy in uniform?"

"Yeah. He looks so macho. Think you could tame him?"

"I doubt it. He doesn't seem the type. He looks more like a dominant man."

"There's lots of guys like that out there girlfriend. Just stop going after the low hanging fruit. Take on a challenge."

"Yeah, you're right. I need a guy who resists being turned into a sub. There should be plenty to choose from when we start college."

"yes indeed. But I'm lazy. I'll take the low hanging fruit. I just want a sub who will get me off any way I wish."

Chapter 13

Steve finished the indy film he'd been working on, a big departure from the action films that had made him both rich and famous. Sometimes he stopped long enough to really see the changes that had gone down in his life these last three and a half years. Before he'd met Lisa, he had always thought he was happy, carefree and happy, always having fun, no commitments, no chains. Lisa had made a nest, a home, a warm place for him to be the real Steve, not the movie star role he played so well that he'd started to think it was really who he was. He was a middle aged man in love with a woman around his own age, something he never would have imagined nor dreamed that he'd actually like. Now, he had to decide how much time to spend at his place and how much at Lisa's. He had long ago discovered that after working hard for weeks, he needed the peace of being in his big, secluded home, and also he really enjoyed his crazy adopted daughter, crazy, weird and fun. Her friend Julie was also quite enjoyable, and quite frankly, had he still been the old Steve, the unattached horn dog Steve, he probably would have made a play for her, maybe, but with her kinks, maybe not.

I'll spend a few days decompressing at home before going back to Lisa's, who is probably so busy putting bad guys in jail that she probably hasn't even missed me. Hopefully the girls haven't trashed the place or organized a marathon party.

Pulling into the driveway, Steve saw the two cars belonging to the girls, so no party, good, and hopefully no big mess. Apparently they'd heard him drive up because both girls came out to greet him. "Welcome home dad." When did she start calling him dad? It wasn't something that happened suddenly, but over time she called him Steve less and less, and dad more. Truthfully, he liked being dad. He actually liked this stage of his life, knowing that with each year things would change, sometimes for the better, other times for the worst, but as long as he had a loving family, it didn't matter.

"Heather, my little girl. How are you, and you Julie, good to see you."

"Mister Longwood, we made a big dinner, more than enough, so please join us."

"Almost too damn good to be true. So, girls, this is your first week of school. What do you think?"

"Too soon to tell," Heather said. "The professors are just going over the syllabus and grading and all that. Did give us a shit load of reading though."

"Yeah, they do that. They spent a lot of years learning all that stuff, so they want you to immerse yourselves in it, to learn to love it."

Hard to believe, he thought as he walked into the house. Spotless, no clothes tossed around, no boys passed out on the sofa, no empty wine bottles. What's the matter with today's youth? He remembered being eighteen, and his parents were always on his case about the messes he'd made.

Steve realized that he hadn't done any in-depth conversations with Julie, and even not many with Heather, so this was the chance to catch up.

Salmon, vegetables al-dente and rice. Steve was impressed. No junk food.

Naturally, the girls wanted to know all about Steve's film work, and he was happy to discuss his work with them, but he really wanted to know more about them and what they were up to. After all, Heather wasn't like the typical girl. He'd known a couple of dominatrix in his years in film, but he never made friends with them. But now, his adopted daughter has obviously committed to that lifestyle, rather than a passing phase in high school.

"Okay, girls, I'm curious. Fill me in on your kinky lifestyle, and remember, I'm not going to judge you, just curious."

Julie was the first to respond. "We made a sub out of the guy who smashed Heather's car, and we both had some fun with him, but now, I guess, he's all mine."

"Why? Did you girls flip a coin or something?"

This time Heather answered. "I just couldn't get

excited about it. I guess it's all too easy. Like these submissive guys seem to recognize my dominant nature and flock to me."

"In other words, no challenge?"

"Yeah, I guess."

"As you may know, in my business, there are all kinds. The freaky and odd seem to be attracted to the movie business, and from what I've seen, men run through the entire spectrum, from total machos to totally submissive. Somewhere on that spectrum is the challenge you're looking for, but don't spend too much time on it. Many people fail out of college the first year because they're too damn busy having fun."

"Yeah, dad. Julie and I have discussed it, and we agree that our education comes before boys. I mean, we can get them pretty much anytime we wish."

Steve laughed. "I hear that. Before I met Lisa I could pretty much get any woman I wanted, star power is even better than good looks."

Julie said, "But, Mr. Longwood, you are pretty good looking for your age."

"My age? Ouch. But thank you, I guess, and please just call me Steve."

Since the girls didn't have classes the next morning and were not going anywhere, Steve opened a bottle of good Zin, and the three of them settled down in the spacious living room and talked well into the night.

Later that night, as the girls were getting ready to go to bed, Julie said. "Your dad, Steve, is a pretty cool guy. He seems to get us, and no judgments."

"I think being with mom has made him a better man, but that's just my feminist instincts talking."

"Wake up girls. Time to rise and shine."

Steve was in the hall, between the girls' rooms, talking loud enough so that he couldn't be ignored.

"Why are you waking us up so early dad?"

"Your mom hasn't seen you all week, and she misses you, told me you girls should get there for breakfast. You don't want to disappoint her, do you?"

That was the magic word for Heather. Disappointing mom was a line she wouldn't cross. To hurt the woman who had saved her was unthinkable. "Thanks dad, we're on it. Julie, we have to go."

A quick cup of coffee and off they went, headed

down highway one. As they drove through Malibu, Heather saw Sage's house and mentioned to Julie that one of her subs lived there, but she'd been too busy to see him.

"Wanna stop?"

"No way. He's just a sub, and there are plenty of them. Only one mom, so no, not going to stop even for a moment."

Lisa had everything ready to cook, and she was relaxing in her robe with a cup of coffee, watching the morning news when the girls pulled into the driveway.

First the hugs and then breakfast, and the girls sat at the kitchen bar while Lisa cooked and asked them about their first week of college.

"Busy, but not much fun yet," Julie said.

"Tons of reading," added Heather.

"Multiply all that by at least five times and you'll have law school, so count yourselves lucky."

"Law school," Julie mused. "Hadn't thought of that. Maybe something to consider."

"Not me," Heather added. "I'll be lucky if I make it through a masters degree. Oh, yeah, dad said he be along a bit later. Says he misses you."

"I miss him too. He's been gone for a couple weeks, and absence makes, well you know."

"You two are lucky. I mean, like you totally love each other, and that's so cool."

"I think both of you are mature enough to find real love, but don't be in a hurry. Get your degrees first." She was interrupted by the phone. "Hi honey. Heather says you'll be coming over soon." There was a pause. "On the road. Good. Miss you."

After breakfast Julie had to leave to visit her parents, and Heather settled in for a reading assignment. Steve and Lisa decided to take a walk on the beach, a romantic thing they both enjoyed, hand in hand, two people in love.

"Steve, I've been feeling kind of out of sorts lately."

"In what way sweetheart?"

"Hard to say, just low energy, kind of weak, tired."

"Probably nothing, but you haven't had a check up since we first got together. I think you need to make an appointment with your doctor."

"I will, but you know how busy I am at work."

"Work is important, but not as important as your health. I get a check up every year, and I feel better knowing I'm in good health. Promise you'll make an appointment."

"Yes, sure."

Steve wasn't convinced she was serious, but he knew enough about her to not press it, hoping the suggestion would lead to something, would ferment in her mind until she took action, and once she decided on action, she'd always follow through.

Chapter 14

By two weeks into the school year, both girls were falling into a routine, Julie still playing with her new sub, Heather still focused on school, not men. But then Julie, while sitting around Steve's living room said, "I've been looking in the mirror, and I don't like what I see."

"How so?"

"I'm starting to look soft, little places where fat is creeping in. I've always been lean, and now I have the body of a thirty-year old."

Heather was half listening, semi working on a school paper. "Most thirty-year olds still look good."

"That's not the point. The university has a gym, and I'm going to start working out, get myself back in shape."

"Have at it. I'm happy to walk and swim, and don't have much time to sweat in the gym."

"You'll change your mind after I get fit."

True to her word, Julie started working out three to four days a week, starting with light weights and the stationary bike, but soon she saw another girl pumping heavy weights, with a muscular body, and Julie told herself she wanted to look that way, so she started increasing the weights. Soon she started seeing more definition, and it was like a drug, addictive. She set herself a goal, to be more buff than that other girl who already had a good head start on her. Yet, Julie thought about her mom, strong, well muscled, even though she didn't lift weights, so Julie figured she had the right genes. Interest started to become obsession, and she checked herself in the gym mirror after every workout, gauging her progress. One day, after she did a set of dead-lifts, she watched a guy try to lift it, but had to take a couple of plates off.

Oh my god, she thought. I'm stronger than some of the guys. Then she had this fleeting thought of not only dominating men with her personality, but dominating them physically, and the thought got her totally sexually excited.

Even though Julie was obsessing about her workouts, she was still using the guy who had damaged Heather's car, and the guy was obviously awed by how buff she was getting, asking to touch her bicep and her quads. Guys, it seemed, not only like to be dominated, but they get off on girls stronger than them, at least some of the guys.

Even at the gym, guys who never noticed her before started watching her lift, obviously with admiring looks, and it made her feel so powerful in every way. Watch out you puny mortal men, she thought, a force of nature is coming your way.

Heather was busy trying to keep up with the reading in her classes, and she was finally starting to take interest in submissive men again. She had discovered that being up front was the best, most expeditious way to go. If a guy showed any interest, she would come right out with it: "I'm a dominant woman and only date submissive boys, so if that's not you, best keep looking."

The majority of the men backed off right away, but a few almost literally threw themselves at her feet. She started having a stable of three subs at a time, dropping one and picking up another periodically, not keeping them long enough to get attached to them. It was always better without any emotional baggage. As long as she could consider them toys, she was emotionally safe, in control, untouchable.

Julie's schedule was getting to her, watching her friend get muscular, and so, reluctantly, Heather started going to the gym, not with anything like the dedication of her friend, not enough to get big or strong, but she liked the definition, the fact that her curves had enough definition to make her look athletic, which in reality, she wasn't. She was uninterested in sports, bike riding, tennis and all that crap. Swimming and a half hour workout was enough for her.

On night while cooking dinner, Julie said that going back to Santa Monica on the weekends meant two days without working out, so she found a cheap gym membership near home, one that had a special rate for weekends only. "For a few bucks more, I can include you."

"No thanks Julie. When I'm home, I want to optimize my time with mom, plus catching up on homework. I'm surprised you have so much free time."

"My classes are pretty easy this semester, but I suspect that they'll get more difficult soon enough. In the mean time, I'm trying to get the most out of my free time. I'm almost embarrassed to say this, but I'm considering getting into a body building competition next year."

"Don't be embarrassed. I think that's really cool, not for me of course, but great for you buff babe."

Steve came in one day and saw Julie in a tank top. "Good going girl. Looks like you've become a total gym rat."

"You approve?"

"Of course. Even though it's not as important these days, being buff was part of my job description for years. The women who attend action films want the leading men to be buff and rather sexy. I was never as dedicated as Hugh Jackman, but had to look good. Love handles equals far fewer parts."

"You still look good for an old guy."

"Mid forties, little girl, not anywhere near an old guy."

Chapter 15

As the old saying goes, time flies when you are either having fun or being super busy, and for these two girls, it was a bit of both. The holidays were upon them, with only weeks left in the semester and final exams rapidly approaching.

Heather was starting to get concerned about Lisa. Mom was looking pale and had lost weight without dieting, and she was tired much of the time. "Mom. Get to a doctor and get a good checkup, please, if not for yourself, for those of us who love you."

Lisa had been meaning to get that check up, but she'd kept putting it off due to her work load and possibly because she was afraid of getting bad news, but now that Heather had started pressuring her, she made the appointment With her long time doctor and friend, Heidi Gardner. Full check up with blood work, and then the doctor ask when she'd had her last mammogram. Heather couldn't remember, so Heidi scheduled one for the next day, telling Lisa to take the damn day off if necessary. "I'm your doctor and your friend and from both directions, I want you on this now."

In a compromise, Lisa scheduled it first thing in the morning so that she could still get all her work done. Even though she considered mammograms uncomfortable, in fact, painful, that's not the reason she had put them off, but rather that her life was so full, so busy that she simply got busy and forgot.

As soon as the mammogram was over, Lisa put it out of her mind, knowing Heidi, her doctor would call her with the results. Back to work again, but having to push herself to get things done. Damn, she thought, why am I so damn tired.

A few days later Lisa got a call from her doctor. "I've got the results from your mammogram, and you need to come in today if possible."

"That sounds bad."

"Not good, but we'll talk about it when you arrive. Come in as soon as you can, and I'll clear my schedule."

"Shit," she shouted. "I've got cancer."

Steve, who happened to be home at the time and was in the other room, heard her shout and came in. "Did I hear you say cancer?"

"Heidi didn't say so, but she wants me in right away. I have so much to do at work."

"Screw work, babe. This sounds serious. Get dressed and I'll drive you to her office."

"You don't need to."

"I want to. I want to be there for whatever news she has. You're the love of my life, and I'm worried sick about you."

Steve waited impatiently in the outer office while Lisa consulted with her doctor, for what seemed an endless amount of time. Then Lisa came out, her face ashen, followed by doctor Heidi, who motioned Steve to follow her.

"Lisa, you should have had a mammogram months ago, but now it has progressed quite far. The good news is we can likely save your life, but I can't imagine how we can save your breasts. Every way I look at this, it comes up radical mastectomy. Then there will be chemo and radiation and a very long, rough recovery. I'm sorry, but I have to give it to you straight."

Lisa listened, but was focused on her life being saved, the rest felt like lead sinkers dropped on her, engulfing her entire body. Steve was devastated. He never fully realized how much she had taken over his life, his heart and soul until now, fearing he might lose her, briefly remembering how much simpler life was when he had no one to care for, simpler but empty, something he wouldn't have realized four or five years ago. Mortality and connection flirted with a deep feeling of emptiness, of the possibility of loss, of the realization that all his fame and money would mean nothing without the love of his life. He was numb as Heidi was going over what will be happening in the very near future, the operation, the chemo, the radiation, the long recovery. He kept replaying her words, "we can likely save your life." Likely, not positively, no guarantees, no sudden miracles.

Lisa, after absorbing the shock of her diagnosis, started thinking in a maternal way about Heather and how deep the connection was. How would this seemingly strong young woman react to this? She dreaded having this conversation, but she knew she could not put it off. She called Heather that evening, after Heather's classes were over for the day. "I got some bad news today, and I need to tell you about it, but don't react until I finish."

That was all it took to focus Heather's attention. "What is it mom?"

"Breast cancer, but it looks like they can save my life. It looks positive, so don't freak out honey."

Heather was stuck on "looks like they can save my life," not they can cure me. To Heather it sounded like she might lose the one person in her life who really mattered, and the thought of being without Lisa was like dropping through a trap door into eternal darkness. "Oh my god, mom. I'll jump in the car and be right there."

No you won't; finish your week, do your assignments and come down on the weekend as usual. Nothing will change in the next two days. I will explain everything to you then."

Heather reluctantly agreed, but try as she might, she couldn't concentrate on her studies, images of attending her mom's funeral kept pushing into her mind. Fear took her directly to Lisa's death without considering the odds, which were usually pretty good for this type of cancer.

Heather's basic biology class was a stadium class with upwards of one hundred students, and she really didn't know anyone except a pleasant young man named Ted, who always kept a seat open for her, as she arrived just at the bell. She hadn't thought much about him, what with her classes and mom on her mind, but he was nice enough, close to six foot, sandy colored hair and an open, likable face, and it seemed that he was interested in her. She considered trying to find out if he was a submissive, but she simply hadn't gotten around to it. But, since he seemed eager to impress her, she figured he might just submit to her when she decided to make her move, but for now he was a pleasant guy who always held a seat for her.

She walked into the auditorium and he waved to

her, pointing to the empty seat. They exchanged greetings and settled in to listen to the lecture, but with Lisa on her mind, Heather could hardly concentrate, something Ted noticed right away. "Is something wrong Heather?"

"What? Oh it shows. My mom called last night; breast cancer, and I'm worried."

"So sorry to hear that, but that type has a high success rate. Your mom can likely beat it."

"I hope so, but she waited so long between exams. I guess it grew."

"Hopefully it didn't metastasize."

"I don't know, but I'll leave right after my last class Friday."

"If there is anything I can do, here's my number." He scribbled it down on a note pad and handed it to her.

She didn't see what he could possibly do for her, but she appreciated the gesture. He was a nice boy, and she liked that.

Her overnight bag was packed, along with her homework, and when the class ended at three o'clock, she was out the door and to her car in minutes, jumping on the road and pushing it toward home and her mom.

She had already told Julie the night before, and her friend asked if she should come along. Heather thought about it for a few moments and decided it would be better to go alone this trip, and Julie said not to worry about anything else, so any problems, just ask. She would go home to her mom, but the next morning. She always worked out on Friday after class, something that had become an obsession.

Chapter 16

Heather promised herself that she'd be positive and smiling and encouraging when she got to her mom's, but seeing her pale and thin made Heather break down and cry as she hugged her mom, deep sobs rising up uncontrollably, the thought of losing her almost too much to consider. She kept telling herself to get in control, to be strong for her mom, but she couldn't stop crying.

"Heather dear, please calm down. I'm doing okay, and the doctor is being very positive. Sit down, have a cup of coffee to calm you, and let's talk."

"Right mom. I'm sorry. I didn't think I'd get so damn emotional."

Heather sat down, catching her breath as Lisa brought in two cups of coffee, handed one to Heather and sat down next to her. "I'll tell you all I know at the moment, but there will be more in a few days. I'll lose both breasts. No way to save them, but with chemo and radiation, Heidi, my doctor, says I will very likely beat it. It won't be fun, but in the end, I'll be alive, and that's important. I have too much to do and too much love to give you and Steve, so I don't plan to die anytime soon."

Heather had calmed down and was able to talk to Lisa. "Mom, you're the toughest person I know. If anyone can beat this, you can. I can drop out of school and take care of you full time."

"Absolutely not. You will go to school, study hard, get good grades and see me on the weekends. I will not be responsible for you dropping out of school."

Heather started to object, but Lisa insisted that it was not open for discussion. "Remember I can talk a jury into putting someone away for life, so don't talk back to me little girl."

"Yes, mom, but you won't mind if I call you every night, just to see how you are and cheer you up?"

"I can live with that. You know how much I love hearing about your school, you classes and all that."

"How is Steve taking it?"

"Not very well. You know, the strong, macho types are the ones who are fragile, and I'm surprised how hard he's taking this. He called his producer and said he was dropping out of the film, even though it's half way done. That can't be good for his career, but he doesn't care. He said that he had enough money, and if he never worked again, so be it."

"Damn it Mom, you'll be living with a house husband. I hope you can train him to iron clothes."

They both got a laugh out of this, and that broke the tension. The conversation then became normal, and Lisa wanted to know all about school, and she asked if Heather was making any new friends.

Heather realized that she really hadn't connected with anyone except perhaps Ted, so she mentioned the nice boy in her class.

"Not one of your subs?"

"No mom. Don't really have time for them right now, but I don't know if he's the type, and I really don't want to think about anything other than classes and you right now."

"Well, a friend is good. You could always use more of them."

"Oh, did I tell you about what Julie is up to?" Lisa shook her head. "She's really gotten into pumping iron, and I can see the difference already. She's gotten really buff, and she is considering becoming a serious body builder. I'm no weakling, but she's easily twice as strong."

"Bring her over. I'd like to see her. I had a gym membership for years, and I was getting pretty strong, particularly in the squat. I could squat more than most of the guys, but that was a long time ago in my twenties."

"Oh, before you got old and gray?" They both laughed.

Heather insisted on cooking dinner, doing the dishes, vacuuming the carpet and dusting the furniture. Lisa sat on the couch, sipping wine and watching her. "I love the service. I should have gotten cancer long ago. You are going to spoil me."

"As a matter of fact, I'm going to spoil the hell out of you all weekend, every weekend, and I'll leave dad a list of things to do during the week. You know men need detailed instructions."

"I've giving him instructions, but it wouldn't hurt for you to follow up with him. He really wants to be able to do something to help."

That night in her room, awake, staring up at the ceiling, the glow of a street light in the window, her mind racing, Heather tried to imagine Lisa being well and back to her old self. She thought about praying, but soon realized she didn't believe it would do a bit of good, so she just tried to think positive thoughts, healing energy and all that stuff, as she slowly drifted off to sleep.

Steve had been out shopping for things for Lisa, and by the time he got home, Heather had gone to bed, so rather than disturb her, he poured some wine and curled up on the couch with Lisa, putting his arm around her, holding her close and whispering desperate words of love. They fell asleep on the couch, TV still on, wrapped in each other's arms.

In the morning it seemed like old times, the three of them in the sunny kitchen, coffee, eggs and bacon, toast and jelly, soft music in the background. For a moment Heather thought that maybe it had all been a bad dream, that mom was well, and they were a typical happy family. Steve tried to put on a positive face, but it was clear how deeply worried he was, how stressed, how completely out of sorts he was, and Heather wanted to comfort him, to comfort her, to try to be strong for everyone she loved.

Later that day when Lisa took a nap, Heather and Steve started making plans, plans were a way to put off the dread and push aside the possibility of Lisa's death. Plans were also necessary as Lisa had always kept things going at home, with Steve gone often for weeks filming a movie, and Heather off at school. They were determined that Lisa would have no worries, no responsibilities, no stress, which, and they probably realized it, wasn't really a possibility. It did, however, give them the feeling they were helping Lisa survive and heal.

"I will be here, and if I'm in Montecito, Lisa

will be with me. No more nights apart." Steve was establishing himself as the devoted husband and possibly devoted father. He'd come a long way in the last few years.

Heather felt closer to him now than in any time in the past. She started to realize his depth, something he'd kept to himself most of his life. That night Heather dreamed that she was at Lisa's funeral, and had to give a eulogy, but when she got up to talk, no sound came out, She just mouthed silent words. She awoke in a cold sweat.

Heather was up early, fixing breakfast for the family, letting the smell of sizzling bacon wake her folks up. Then as they came in, she handed them coffee and pointed to the food on the table. She felt good, really complete and at peace for perhaps the first time. She was part of this family, an important part, and it was up to her to make everything work, everyone happy or at least comfortable.

After breakfast and Steve insisted on doing the dishes, he suggested to Lisa that they take a walk, if she felt up to it. She did, and they dressed and walked down to the beach and strolled along the sand, watching the surfers, and the people on the wharf, walking slowly, hand in hand, two pleasant people obviously deeply in love. Gulls chirped above them and children played on the sand, mothers carefully watching. The world seemed perfect, and it was hard to believe that this cancer might bring this perfect world crumbling around them. "You have made a walk on the beach seem more exciting than a hundred movie studio parties. Thank you for being you."

Rather than answer, Lisa squeezed his hand, looked up and smiled at him, and that made tears of both joy and sorrow start to flow. What would he possibly do if he lost her. He would not want to do another film, TV show or any of it. That part of his life was over. Now it was Steve Longwood, family man, devoted husband and father. It was also Steve Longwood with a paid off huge home in Montecito and a few million in the bank. There was no longer a need to work, other than for the gratification.

Heather spent the weekend doing all she could to make Lisa's life easier, along with getting a deeper understanding of Steve, who was far more than an action hero in the movies. The man had interests and was conversant in many areas, which impressed Heather.

Heather had considered Steve to be dad, only with quotation marks implied, but now she was thinking of him as dad with no conditions or considerations. She had two real, at least in her thinking, parents, and she would have been happy if Lisa had been well. "Are they going to operate Mom?"

"Yes dear and pretty soon. Timing is apparently important."

It was Sunday morning, sun streaming in the kitchen window, the two of them in their robes, sipping coffee while Steve was out for a morning jog. "Do you have a date for it yet?"

"Heidi will let me know sometime this coming week. I don't know what I'll do about work."

"Mom, to hell with work. Your health is the most important thing. Even if you lose your job, Steve has all the money you two will ever need."

"That's not the point. My job is more than a job. It's who I am, what I love doing, how I make a difference."

"Then concentrate on getting well, so you can go back and put lots more bad guys in jail."

Lisa gave her a big hug. "Yes, my worrying girl. I'll do just that."

"Please call me the minute you have a date for the operation."

"Well, sure, I'll try to do that, maybe not immediately, but you know."

Heather could read this hesitation, thinking mom wouldn't want to disrupt her studies, so she would talk to Steve and get him to promise.

Heather would return to Montecito sometime Sunday evening, get a good night's sleep and make the half hour drive to class in the morning, but this time she elected to stay Sunday night, get up before dawn and head straight to class. She took Steve aside that evening and insisted that he inform her as soon as mom had her operation scheduled.

Steve realized that there was little he could say to the girl, insistent as she was, so he agreed. The next day he got the opposite view from Lisa. "I don't want her coming down in the middle of the week to fret over me and miss her classes. Don't call her with the operation date. I'll call her when I'm home or on the weekend, whichever comes first."

Heather got a text from Sage, saying he missed his Mistress and hoped she would come and do whatever she wished with him. He was not only hooked on being a submissive, but he had gotten into this to write a book about the BDSM lifestyle, and he needed more experience. Both issues seemed equally important, him being quite passionate about being a writer and also a submissive. The text came as she was driving through Malibu, and she thought about stopping, at least for a minute, but then she realized that she couldn't get excited about seeing him or any other sub. Sex was fine, but her mom was all she had on her mind.

She hadn't been at the Montecito house since leaving for school Friday morning, and it was now Monday late afternoon, and she was ready for a hot shower and some study time, perhaps being able to take her mind off Lisa long enough to study. Julie was already home, doing pushups when Heather walked in, not girl pushups but regular ones, and many of them. Heather wondered if she were able to do them, and Julie said, "Come on down here girlfriend, and knock out a few."

Heather sighed and dropped to the floor, got in position and let herself down on the carpet before pushing back up with much effort. She managed to do three, the last one not quite all the way. Julie shook her head and said, "We have to get you in shape, but first, how's your mom?"

"She's being really brave, probably for me, but I know she's worried. I mean, like they want to operate right away."

Julie jumped to her feet in a single bound, the tank top showing off her broad shoulders. "You know I'm here for you and for her. Whatever you need. Just ask."

They hugged and Heather started to cry, Julie holding her, not saying a word, just letting her friend let it out, purge the painful emotions.

In an effort to change the subject, Heather asked Julie about her boys, and Julie said she was into something new. She was only going after slender guys, not boys with muscles, but lean and not very strong. "It's such a turn on to be with a guy who I can physically overpower. It turns them on too. It's sort of double domination, the physical part adding to the excitement. One guy actually begged me to flex for him and let him touch my bicep. What a total turn on."

Heather was happy for her friend, but at the moment, it wasn't something she would want to talk to her friend about.

Julie sensing a lack of enthusiasm said, "Well, you have other things on your mind, and when your mom is healthy again, you can go back to enjoying your toys."

Each day Heather listened for a call, thinking mom must have a surgery date by now, but nothing. Her calls to her mom and to Steve were unanswered. Finally, she sent Steve a text: "If I don't hear anything in the next hour, I'm coming down."

Steve called a few minutes later. "I'm sorry dear, but Lisa said not to tell you. She wants you to concentrate on your studies."

"So when is the operation scheduled?"

There was an uncomfortable silence for what seemed a full minute. "it, well, it was yesterday, and she's doing fine and will be home in a couple days."

Heather freaked out. "What the fuck, Steve. You promised to tell me so I could be there."

"I got conflicting instructions, and as much as I wanted to call you, Lisa said absolutely not. There is nothing you can do except for missing class, and besides, she'll be home this weekend."

"That's two days away. I'm on my way home and will not be put off." Before Steve could respond, Heather had hung up, grabbed a change of clothes, leaving her books on the table and jumped in her car and sped off toward Santa Monica.

Steve was at the hospital, where he'd been almost constantly. He walked into Lisa's room and said, "Your daughter is obstinate, and she's on her way here. Nothing I could do to stop her."

Lisa shook her head, but being on pain pills, she dozed off to sleep in a few minutes.

Heather pulled over for a bottle of water and called doctor Heidi. "What hospital is mom at?"

She stormed into the hospital, demanding to know what room Lisa was in, and then, not willing to wait for the elevator, ran up the two flights and into her mom's room.

"Mom, how are you doing?"

"I'm fine Heather, and you didn't need to come. I'll be home this weekend, so you didn't have to blow off your classes. I don't ever want to think I've messed up your education."

"My professors know my situation, and they'll excuse me for a day or so. Mom, tell me everything, what did the doctors say about your recovery."

"You know how doctors are. It's never cut and dried. Said my odds of full recovery are close to eighty percent."

"That's still kind of scary. They won't give you anything more positive?"

"That's not how it works dear. They have to give it to me straight, and I'm glad they did. I have something to fight for, and eighty percent is good odds."

Heather sat by Lisa's bed until the pain pills made her drowsy, and she drifted off to sleep. Heather got up and went to find Steve. She was going to say something about the odds and how weak mom looked, but the tears started to flow, and she buried her face in Steve's jacket and sobbed. Visiting hours ended, and the staff had to push Steve and Heather out, telling them they could come back at seven in the morning, which was only ten hours away.

Back at the house, Heather could see the stress written all over Steve's face. He poured a big tumbler of wine, and Heather said she would need at least that much. The two of them sat in the silent living room, sipping their wine and saying very little until Heather, not used to drinking more than a glass, fell asleep on the couch. Steve brought in a blanket and covered her, picking up his wine, turning off the light and going into the bedroom where he sat in the dark, drinking wine and quietly crying.

They were at the hospital the following morning at seven, but apparently Lisa was out of her room, some kind of test or something, and they had to wait. Finally, she was wheeled back into the room, looking pale and sick. "Radiation, and I don't feel very good, so I'm not going to be good company."

Heather and Steve tried to smile and cheer her up, but soon Lisa drifted off to sleep, and the nurse said it would be better to let her rest, so please come back this evening.

Over breakfast Steve laid down the law. "Lisa will not hear of you missing school. You'll come down on the weekends and bring your studies, and that's not open to debate. In fact you are not welcome during the week, so don't even think about it. Now, all I want to hear is yes dad."

Defeated, Heather sighed and said, "Yes dad."

Heather wanted to stay Sunday night, but Steve insisted that she go back to Montecito. "Make sure my house is locked up safe, and don't forget to water the plants, and tell Julie to make her bed. Now, bye bye little girl."

Julie wanted to know everything, and so they talked for hours Sunday evening, finally hanging it up and going to bed late. Julie tried to keep Heather's spirits up, saying how strong Lisa is and how she can beat this easily.

Monday morning was the biology intro class, held in an auditorium, and as usual Heather saw that Ted was holding a seat for her. If I was in the mood for another sub, Ted would be a good choice, but I can't get into it right now. However, he immediately saw Heather's distressed mood and asked how her mom was doing.

It was all Heather could do no to cry in front of him, something no self-respecting dom would ever do. "She looks so weak and fragile."

"Everyone looks weak and fragile after an operation. I bet she'll look much better next weekend. Could I buy you a coffee after class?"

Heather looked hard at him, his expression saying he really wanted to help, that he cared about Heather and by extension, her mom. It took a moment, but finally, "Sure, what the hell."

They strolled over to the student union, chatting about the biology lesson. They poured coffee, grabbed a snack and found a table in a corner. Ted wanted to know about Lisa and how she was doing, and Heather, trying to keep it together in front of a male, started talking as if were a simple topic of conversation, something Ted obviously saw right through. It was clear he wanted to say something personal to her, but was uncomfortable attempting. Finally, he said, "You know I like you Heather, I mean, like more than just a friend, but nothing I want to push or anything."

"That's sweet Ted, but there's something I need to tell you up front. I'm a dominant woman, and I'm only interested in submissive men. You understand what that means?"

"I think so. I do believe a strong woman can, should lead, but I'm not into the kinky stuff I've heard about."

"Well, right now I have too much on my mind, but for now, friends."

"Yes, friends, which is good, since I don't want to call you Mistress Heather."

"We will cross that bridge when we get there my friend. In the mean time, I appreciate your friendship."

They changed the subject, to Ted's relief, and again started talking about biology. "You know," he said, "there isn't much biological difference between men and women, besides sex organs and that. I could never understand how society has assigned different roles and gender expectations."

"I feel exactly the same way, and I like that you feel that way. I think we will get along just fine." Then she gave him a sly smile and added, "with minimal training apparently."

He laughed nervously, not really sure if she were kidding.

As much as Heather didn't want any complications, she found herself going for coffee after class every session, discussing biology, his plans to be a scientist, but staying clear of the subject of sex. It was nice to have a male friend, her first, Steve not really counting.

It was comfortable and a distraction from Lisa and studies, a peaceful island in a sea of uncertainty, a place of calm to keep the demons at bay. As much as Heather was reluctant to admit it, these conversations over coffee with Ted were therapeutic. They were not, however, romantic or sexual in the least.

She did, from time to time, connect with a sub for a bit of kinky fun, but less and less now that between studies and Lisa, Heather had little free time. She didn't see how Julie did it, at least an hour a day in the gym, two subs, a full schedule of classes and time to be Heather's best friend. Although, had it not been for Lisa's cancer, she could probably keep just as hectic a schedule.

Chapter 17

Heather had fallen into a routine, heading back to Santa Monica Friday afternoon, back to Montecito sometime Sunday evening. Heather enjoyed driving at night, as less traffic on the road, and it didn't bother her driving in the dark. During the week, it was her classes, coffee with Ted twice a week, class lectures, reading assignments, homework, quizzes, a weekly trip for groceries and attempting to keep Steve's house neat and clean, something Julie was a huge help with.

Lisa was now going through chemo and radiation, and she'd lost her hair and a fair amount of weight. She had little energy, none for sex, and that was fine with Steve, as when he looked at her, he felt sorry for her, rather than passion. He was content to simply hold her at night until she fell asleep. At that point, sometimes he'd fall asleep with her, and other times He'd get up and just pace around the house in the dark, finally settling down to read until he was tired amd could no longer keep his eyes open.

Steve wasn't going to Montecito very often. Lisa wasn't feeling like traveling, and she was more comfortable at home. He told the girls it was up to them to keep the place up, stocked with food and to at least leave a bottle or two of wine for when he did show up. Heather and Julie were settled in comfortably, and they invited Nadia to visit, but since they were gone most weekends, and Nadia had school during the week, it didn't happen often. However, Julie, not wanting to be in the way at Lisa's place and not feeling the need to see her parents every weekend, had Nadia up on some weekends, when they both trolled for submissive guys, which seemed to be plentiful, and the guys all thought Nadia was a college student, which she never denied.

When Nadia saw Julie in a tank top, she was blown away by the changes in her friend. "What's with all the bulging muscles?"

I've gotten really into body building, and it's like an addiction, but a good, healthy one. Also, it's such a rush making my subs arm wrestle me, letting them think they are winning, and then taking them down."

"I'm sure there are lots of really strong guys out there who would beat you."

"Sure, but I'm only into the weak, thin guys, not anyone who works out or anything like that. I got this one little guy who I make kiss my bicep, and he loves it. I call it double submissive. When I take him over my knee and spank him, he actually cums."

Nadia started thinking about that, how it might feel to dominate a guy, not just with her personality but physically, and it felt exciting. "There's a weight room at school, and I'm going to get in there every day until I'm a big as you. Then I'll only take on subs I can beat arm wrestling."

"Make sure you eat a high protein diet to build muscle. Look on YouTube for videos on building muscle. You've got the right body, so you should start seeing results soon."

Nadia flexed her biceps, and while not big, at least there was some definition.

"My gym allows guests, so let's go over there now, and I'll show you some lifts."

The girls ended up spending most of the afternoon at the gym, and by the time they got back to the house, Nadia was so tired, she could hardly move, but once she flopped down on the couch, she sighed and said, "God, I feel so fucking good. If you have some subs around here, have them come over."

Julie made a couple of calls and soon there was a knock at the door. Two thin but handsome young men were at the door, looking eager to please Mistress Julie. She lead one of them over to Nadia and said, "This one's yours girlfriend."

Nadia didn't even get up. Instead she motioned him over and said, "I'm sore from working out, and I need first a massage and then I'll need my pussy licked. Do you think you can handle that?"

He responded enthusiastically. Then she said that if he didn't do a good job, she would take him over her knee and give him a spanking.

The boys were shy about servicing the girls in

front of each other and asked if they could go to the bedrooms for privacy, but the girls said no. "It's a turn on being able to watch each other get served, so you boys will have to perform in front of each other. If you are good boys and do as you are told, we might let you orgasm. You want to orgasm don't you?"

Like pet puppies, they both nodded, and the girls ordered them to get naked, which, in spite of their embarrassment, they did. Then the girls enjoyed using them all evening, finally sending them home after midnight.

"That was an awesome day." Nadia was sprawled out on the thick carpet. "I got off like four or five time this evening."

"Me too," Julie said. "I loved it when they begged to be allowed to cum."

"Yeah, and you and I saying we were thinking about it, letting them sweat it for a long time before we consented. I love that kind of power."

Julie got a text from Steve, saying he figured that the girls were getting into his wine supply, so he arranged for two of the wineries he was a member of to double his order. "More wine on the way girls, but moderation or I will lock it all up and you'll be reduced to sodas and water."

The girls were practicing moderation, and the evening routine on school nights was to finish all the reading and homework and then have one glass before bed, a glass of wine and some conservation about school, family, subs and whatever else floated up in the peaceful Montecito night. However, when Nadia was visiting Julie had to keep an eye on her, as she seemed to really like to drink, and had to be reminded that moderation was a hard rule in the house. "I'm worried," she said to Heather one evening. I think Nadia has a possible alcohol addiction problem."

"You gotta set limits on her. If her parents find out she's getting drunk here, and then Steve finds out, we will lose our wine privileges. Steve has enough on his plate with mom, and I don't want him pissed at us for letting Nadia get shit faced."

Fortunately for Nadia, her parents didn't keep any alcoholic beverages in the house, and she wasn't able to get to Montecito more than a couple times a month, so any desire she had for alcohol was frustrated until she got the idea to get a sub who was old enough to buy it. So, she went over to his place after school frequently, had him service her and drank more than what was good for her, and she had him pick her up and drive her home. To get stopped for being drunk at seventeen would have been bad news, and her parents would have grounded her for weeks or months. On those nights, she went straight to her room and started to do homework, or at least as well as she could in her compromised condition. Mouthwash and mints kept up her illusions while having dinner.

However, one day when she called her sub, Andrew, he said that his car was in the shop and he couldn't pick her up. Desperate for a drink, Nadia got in her car, drove over, played with Andrew for awhile, had several glasses of wine and then said she had to get home before her parents came home. It was only three miles, but miles in the heart of town, and a police officer saw her weave and pulled her over. She was double the legal limit and was promptly arrested and her parents called. She refused to say where she got the booze, not that she cared much about Andrew, but she didn't want her supply cut off. When her parents grilled her about it, she said she talked some guy into going into the store and buying her a bottle. A trip to juvenal court, some community service and heavy restriction at home, and Nadia was cut off from Andrew and from trips to Montecito. Her parents insisted she go to Alcoholics Anonymous, so there she was in a meeting with really gross older people with serious addiction problems, and she felt she wasn't one of these losers.

"Julie, I've been busted, so don't know when I'll be able to get up there again."

Julie said she felt bad about that, but in reality she was relieved. Nadia had become a bit of a problem with Steve's wine. Naturally Andrew regretted what had happened, as he had gotten into the whole BDSM thing with her and wasn't anxious for it to end. He suggested he might come to her place early enough to be gone when her parents got home. She was good with that but only if he brought wine.

That worked for a couple of weeks until her parents came home one evening to find her passed out on the couch. This time she was shaken as her parents threatened to have her locked up, seeing they couldn't control their daughter. It put the fear to her, and the next time she went to an AA meeting, she spoke for the first time.

"My name is Nadia, and I'm an alcoholic. I've been busted by the cops driving home from a boyfriend's place where I had made him buy me wine. I could make him do lots of things for me, but that's not important. Now, my parents no longer trust me and they've threatened to send me to juvenal hall or to my grandmother's place out in the middle of nowhere. All I think about is drinking, and I don't know what to do."

There it was, she had confessed, taken responsibility and had thrown herself on the mercy of the group. After the meeting a young woman, no more than early twenties sat down with her and said she would like to be her sponsor. She told Nadia her story, about getting so drunk she couldn't remember what she had done, how she came up pregnant at eighteen and couldn't even remember what guy was responsible, how she had to get an abortion and was ostracized at school in her senior year, missing the prom, not even bothering to go to her graduation, not being able to hold a job, stay in community college and all the rest until she joined AA and started to turn her life around. Now she was sober two years, had a job, a boyfriend and her own apartment.

Nadia took all this in, seeing herself in this woman's story, thinking about her possible future, and she cried. "Help me."

For the first time Nadia felt helpless. She had always been strong, able to make boys obey her every wish, but now she realized she was helpless against alcohol, and it crushed her self image.

Her new sponsor, Susan, was a tall, slender blond, quite pretty, with a open smile and a disarming manner. Nadia immediately trusted her and knew that she was now in good hands.

Nadia's parents, Sikhs and non drinkers, were pleased that their little girl was getting the help she needed and relieved that they didn't have to disown her, seeing that they had a religious objection to alcohol and couldn't abide a member of the family drinking, let along becoming an alcoholic.

"Julie, I won't be coming up there for awhile. I

have a sponsor in AA and lots of meetings to attend. I haven't had a drink in almost a month."

Julie was sorry that her friend couldn't come up, but she had Heather there during the week, her best friend, and they helped each other with classes and were there to discuss whatever came up. Julie had two subs, both from school, and she had set times to play with them, one during the week, at his place, the other on the weekends in Montecito. Heather had a sub she enjoyed from time to time, but she soon dropped him because of school, her mom and being there for Steve, who was constantly worrying about losing Lisa. Heather realized that at this point in her life, she had two good friends, Julie and Ted, and Ted was her first real male friend, something she wasn't sure how to deal with. Without him totally submitting to her, anything sexual was out of the question, a hard and fast rule. There was also Nadia, who she hadn't seen for weeks.

Not asking herself why, Heather always looked forward to her coffee date with Ted, talking about the biology class and being able to share with him her concerns over her mom. Ted had a way of finding something positive in any situation, and she remembered the boys she had killed, realizing that Ted was the opposite of them, and that she couldn't imagine hurting him physically or emotionally. In fact, she was feeling oddly protective of him.

Heather wasn't one to over think things, so she didn't ask herself about this odd relationship, how she felt about him beyond that the friendship was pleasant, and he was a good sounding board for her concerns. She didn't find him attractive or even someone she would want as a submissive. He was just a nice guy, and the coffee dates were a comfortable, regular part of her week. When she wasn't with him, she didn't think about him, and in fact the only person she thought much about was Lisa.

Chapter 18

Nadia was missing her friends, even though she hadn't seen Heather in weeks. The weekends in Montecito were fun, but there was too much temptation with all the good wine. She also decided to give up Andrew, as he was far too anxious to supply her with alcohol. I'm only seventeen, she thought, yet I'm in AA and will have to go the rest of my life without a glass of wine, beer, whatever. It doesn't seem fair. Julie has her two glasses at night and she's fine. I have two and need two or three more. I've tried, she mused, but once I start, I just can't stop.

Julie was talking to Heather about Nadia one evening, after study time, for their nightly glass of wine. "I think we should take her to lunch one weekend, when we are both in Santa Monica. I think she needs her friends."

"I'm good with that, but have to work it around mom and her needs."

"How is she doing?"

"She's responding to treatment, but it's taken a toll on her. She's thin and weak and the chemo has taken her hair. Sometime I want to cry when I see her, but I have to be brave and positive and all that shit."

"You are doing all you can. If you were religious, I'd suggest praying, but, well."

"Pray to a mythological creature? Doesn't sound too fucking helpful."

Heather and Julie invited Nadia to lunch, and they all realized that it had been awhile since they had all been together, three women with few other friends, three women with common interests, three close friends. The first thing Nadia wanted to know what how Lisa was doing, so Heather filled her in before asking her about her involvement in AA.

"I kind of resented it at first, thinking why me, why do I have to pass every time someone offers me a drink. My sponsor is a great gal, and I even told her about my dominance and that I have subs, and she was just fine with that, saying that it sounded fun dominating men."

Just then a guy walked by, stopped, said hi and waited for a response. Nadia took the bait. "If you want to converse with three dominant women, you'd best get on you knees now."

The guy looked totally shocked, muttered something neither he or the girls understood and just walked away. "Power! Even better than alcohol." Nadia was smiling.

Julie was thinking about Lisa. "Let's all take Lisa and Steve out for dinner, nice place, spend some money, show them a good time."

"Yeah," Heather said. "But we have to work it around mom's good days, and sometimes we don't know until the last minute."

"And it has to be here. It's a problem getting up to Montecito now that my folks have gotten paranoid about my drinking."

They broached the idea with Steve who not only agreed, but said he would kick in something for an even more memorable evening. "I know just the place."

It was a restaurant in Santa Monica that the girls had heard of but hadn't even considered, being that it was very fancy and very expensive. Steve said he knew the owner, so as soon as Lisa was up to it, he'd make a reservation.

It was a wonderful evening. Lisa was feeling stronger, and the girls were upbeat and full of talk about school, friends and a few references to their subs. Steve was happier than they had seen him in weeks. It was strange, Heather thought, that this guy, former leading man, man about town, heartthrob, was now the devoted husband and father. Heather never realized the depth behind that winning smile.

Somehow Sage had found out where they were dining, and he showed up, obviously after several drinks, and he was determined to get Heather to rekindle the relationship. When Heather told him to leave, he got loud and demanding. Steve quietly got up, grabbed Sage by the shoulder and said, "Leave now, or I'll throw you out. Your call buddy."

Sage was about to argue with Steve, but it was clear that Steve wasn't bluffing, and he was still buff and more than capable of tossing Sage out the door. So, after trying to stare Steve down, unsuccessfully, Sage left, and Heather decided that she would never bother with him again.

Lisa insisted that Heather stop worrying about her, that she was responding to treatment, and the prognosis looked good. "I don't like what this is doing to you my sweet child. The stress is showing on your face, in your posture, even in you hair. If you don't relax and stop trying to be everything for me, I'm going to have to confine you to Montecito, including weekends."

"Mom, I can't help worrying, and I'd worry more if I was up there and couldn't see you, not knowing how you were and all that."

"Perhaps," Steve interjected, "it might be a good idea to see that counselor, what was his name? Oh yeah, doctor Williams."

"I don't think he did me much good before, and I doubt he would now."

"Humor me." Lisa said. "It wouldn't hurt to talk to him, just once if it doesn't help."

Heather sighed, realized Lisa had made up her mind, and rather than argue, she said, "Sure, if he can do a weekend appointment."

Although she didn't say anything to Lisa, Heather knew Sean would make himself available any time she wished. She was sure he'd do anything she asked.

"Sean, it's your mistress. How has my little sub been?"

It had been weeks, and Sean knew Heather was away at school, and he was afraid he might never hear from her again, so this was a very exciting surprise. "Your little sub has missed his Mistress."

"Of course you have. I would like to tell you I'm calling about dominating you, but mom wants me to discuss something with you on a professional level. Saturday morning work for you?"

"Yes Mistress. Saturday will be fine. In my office or at home?"

"Don't be a naughty boy. This is about your professional services, but if you give me a good session, I might be inclined to fuck you with that strapon, and I know how much you love that."

"Yes Mistress, I love that. I'll see you Saturday in my office. What time will you be there?"

"I think nine in the morning will do just fine. See you then little sub."

God, I love the power over men, she thought. I'll get some professional help and then maybe have some fun. I wish I could tell all the little girls to put away their dolls and play with the better toys, the boys.

"Okay Mom. I made an appointment with Dr. Williams for Saturday morning. I hope he can help me feel less anxious."

Hoping to cheer Lisa up, Heather put together a small party Friday night, inviting Julie, Nadia, Steve, Megan, D'Wanda and Lisa's assistant in the DA's office. She tried to give Steve some money for wine, but he handed it back, and she picked up snacks, loaded Lisa's favorite bands on the smart speaker and tried to act cheerful, like no one had a care in the world. If I pull this off, she mused, I might go into acting.

They were all sitting around Lisa's living room, drinking wine, except Nadia, who was tempted, but was stopped by Julie. "You know you can't go there girlfriend."

Lisa noticed that Nadia wanted a drink, but couldn't take one, so she asked what was the issue, thinking it was just her age.

"I am an alcoholic. I'm a member of AA, and it really sucks, being only seventeen and having to never touch booze again."

Lisa had more questions, but Nadia didn't want to tell her that the drinking problem started on those Montecito weekends, so she was rather vague about parties and other places she might have had alcohol.

"What do your parents think about your problem?"

"Drinking is against their religion, I guess mine too, although I don't really practice it. So, anyway, they were not at all happy, and I would have been disowned if I hadn't joined AA."

The party ended early, as Lisa, weak from the chemo and radiation, was too tired to stay up. She went off to bed, Steve joining her, and the rest left. The girls decided to go to a local diner for coffee and dessert. "She doesn't look too good," Nadia commented.

Julie looked at Nadia and shook her head, and

Heather said, "Yeah, and it's breaking my heart. I wish the doctors would tell me more."

Julie said she'd been reading up on breast cancer and that even when the prognosis is good, the doctors never want to make promises. Still, everything she'd read indicated that Lisa was likely to recover.

Heather said she thought the mastectomy had hit Lisa pretty hard. She wasn't sure how Steve would handle it if or when she were well enough for intimacy.

Julie shook her head. "Men, so fucking shallow. No wonder I enjoy dominating them. It serves them right."

"Remember girlfriend, we're talking about Steve, one of the really good guys."

"Even good guys can be a total pain in the ass when it comes to their view of women. Dominated men are so much better. Good training is necessary to keep them on the right path."

They all picked up their coffee cups and said they'll drink to that.

Saturday morning, and even though Heather could have been to Sean's office in plenty of time, she decided to be fifteen minutes late just to remind him who was in charge.

"Hi sub. Sorry I'm late, but you know."

"That's okay Mistress. I am here for you."

"Good boy. Mom thinks I'm depressed over her condition and she thinks you can help. Do you think so sub?"

"I hope so Mistress. Tell me about your feelings."

It was going to be one of those forced conversations, talking about and around it, but after a few minutes, and knowing Sean was no emotional threat, Heather found herself opening up and just spilling out all her feelings, how Lisa had saved her four years earlier, how she'd forgiven her for murder, how she'd adopted her."

Sean just let her go, the words tumbling out, the tears flowing. He only had to be there, to listen, to nod occasionally, to produce the right facial expressions, and when she was done, to validate her experiences, to let her know she had made a breakthrough.

Heather caught her breath and realized she had shown her vulnerability, something she would never do in front of a male. She forced herself to be icy and strong again, looked him straight in the eye and said "Thank you for listening. Would you like a reward?"

As much as he wanted to refuse, the idea of being rewarded by his strict mistress was too exciting, and he said yes.

"Bring out the strapon sub, and hurry up."

Sean had anticipated that and had the sex toy in his desk, and quickly pulled it out and said, "Here it is Mistress."

"Good boy. Now, drop your pants and bend over your desk."

He did as she ordered while she took off her jeans and sweater, leaving her panties and bra on, cinched up the strapon, lubed it and grabbed the cheeks of his ass.

"Are you ready to be fucked sub?"

"Yes Mistress, fuck me hard."

She fucked him almost brutally until she heard him orgasm and then collapse on the desk, breathing hard.

"That's my good boy," she said as she pulled it out and slapped him on the ass. "Keep being a good boy, and we'll do this again. You'd like that, right sub?"

"Yes Mistress, I'd love that."

She got dressed, told him to clean the dildo and walked out of his office, feeling much better. He's a worm, she thought, but a pretty good psychologist.

"How was your session with Doctor Williams? " Lisa wanted to know.

"I would have to say it went well Mom. I feel much better now, but I'm still going to hover like the dedicated girl you've taught me to be, and I won't take any argument."

Heather's life settled into a harsh routine: school all week, home after her last Friday class, weekends taking care of Lisa, whether she needed it or not, comforting Steve, who was showing an unexpected vulnerability, and trying to keep up with her friends whenever possible. Julie was easy, as they had their routine in Montecito, but Nadia required making an island of time. The younger girl was closing in on eighteen, and would be graduating mid term, so would be headed to college after the upcoming holiday season.

Heather and Julie had talked her into applying at Cal State Channel Islands, saying there was plenty of room at the Montecito mansion, naturally getting Steve's permission before offering. Soon the three of them would be together, and while both Julie and Nadia would have their subs, Heather had decided that until her mom was well, she wouldn't have time for men for any purpose. And, she took a perverse delight in informing Sean, Sage and the others that she no longer had the time or interest to bother with them.

    Lisa had been able to work for the first part of her treatment, but now, weak from chemo and radiation, she could no longer make it through the work day, and this was the hardest part of this disease. She realized that her self-image was wrapped up in her job, and that not working almost meant not being real, being some sort of wraith, an entity, but not completely solid.

    Heather had been hovering over her every weekend from Friday afternoon to late Sunday, and while she appreciated it, she wished her adopted daughter would spend more of her time having a life, being an eighteen year old college girl, rather than a care giver. Reflecting back over the last almost four years, she could hardly believe the changes in the girl and in their relationship. Heather had been a troubled teen, a serial killer, a hater of all things male, and Lisa had done all she could to put the girl away, so no more boys would die at her hand, but now she couldn't imagine life without her devoted daughter. Certainly, her dominant behavior, her having subs she could command, seemed odd in the least, but now she was realizing that these guys wanted that kind of relationship, that being dominated and humiliated fueled their sexual fantasies. Heather was, in her own weird way, doing these guys a service.

    Having time on her hands, Lisa started researching this sexual kink, learning that there were various degrees of BDSM, from relationships where the woman took the lead in most things to the really weird, whips, spankings, foot worship and all the rest. In doing her research, she started to realized that she and Steve had a very mild version of this kind of relationship. He had come to the point of always putting her first, not making final decisions without checking with her first. He treated her like a queen, essentially worshiping her, which felt really good, but when looked at from the point of view of Heather's lifestyle, it was almost a female led relationship. How, she wondered, did a famous movie start, womanizer, hunk become such a devoted husband. Was it something she did or something she naturally was? It was something she pondered often, having little else to do with herself when able to stay awake. She certainly wasn't any sex object at this point, scars where her breasts used to be, thin and pale, having lost all her hair. She could hardly recognize herself in the mirror any longer.

Lisa was falling asleep early, leaving Heather and Steve to spend the late evenings together, and they were getting to know each other better every weekend. Steve had gone from just a nice guy, movie star and owner of a great place for the girls to stay to someone very interesting, someone multifaceted, someone she could talk to for hours. She quickly learned that while Steve kept up a brave front, he was devastated by Lisa's condition, and in a moment of wine induced openness, he admitted that Lisa had become the driving force in his life, that she had replaced acting as his reason for getting through the day, the literal light in his life.

"It's hard to believe, I mean, a famous movie star and all that. Mom is awesome, but you had such a great life."

"It's called the fantasy life. People read about guys like me and think how great, how romantic, how cool it is to be a star. To tell the truth, I had pretty much no real friends, just those who hang around to say they have a pal who is a big movie star. No one really got to know me before Lisa, and that's a powerful feeling." He poured himself another glass, looked over at Heather and said, "I'm still not sure I should be giving you wine since you are not legally old enough to drink."

Heather looked around, under the coffee table, behind Steve and finally said, "I don't see any cops. I don't think you'll get arrested for contributing to my delinquency. So please, another glass for your wino daughter."

Heather was so glad Steve was married to Lisa. He had the financial and emotional resources to see her through this terrible illness, and Heather was finally thinking of him as totally dad, so much better than the distant dad who raised her, or actually didn't really raise her at all.

As usual, Heather dashed into the biology class at the bell, and as usual Ted had a seat held for her. The professor was explaining how plants and animals share much of their DNA, so we shouldn't think of plants as that much difference. In fact, she pointed out, plants actually plan how they will grow and why. That caught Heather by surprise since she'd always thought of plants as so much different from animals. Ted, on the other hand, was fascinated, leaning over and saying he'd always thought that same thing, and now his instincts have been proven right. After class, over coffee, he was anxious to discuss it, and while Heather really didn't have an opinion, she listened politely to his excited talk.

Finally, as he wound down, he asked her what was going on in her life. She gave him the latest news about Lisa and then told him that her friend Nadia will be graduating mid term and might be coming to school there, and if so, she would be sharing a place with her two best friends.

"Must be a big place if all three of you can live there."

"Yeah. I guess I never mentioned that we're staying in dad's place in Montecito, a huge place with five bedrooms."

"Five bedrooms in Montecito. He must be pretty well off."

"I guess I didn't tell you about him. Steve Longwood, the movie actor."

"No shit! I know who he is. Seen some of his movies. I'd love to hear all about it."

"Well, he married my mom, adopted mom, and he spends some of his time at her place and some at his Montecito place. We have the run of the house, except for the master bedroom suite. We have rules about the place, but he's cool with us enjoying the accommodations. It made it possible for us to go to school here with no housing expenses."

"What about your real parents? You haven't told me anything about them."

"I don't like to talk about them. Dad killed himself, and mom is an alcoholic bum shacking up with some guy, some place."

"Wow, that really sucks, but you've landed nicely on your feet with your adopted parents. Fortunately, I get along with my parents, seeing that I can't afford to move to my own place. Unfortunately, my daily commute is a bitch."

"Even if Nadia moves in, there's still one more bedroom, so maybe I could ask Steve if it's okay. You're a nice guy, and if you did your share of the chores and bought some wine, perhaps we could make room for you."

"And your friends? Are they dominants like you?"

"Oh, yes, but if you'd like I'll instruct them to leave you alone."

"Yeah, that would be good. I'm not sure how I could handle three dominant women. I'd be way outnumbered."

"If anyone ever gets to dominate you, it would be me, but with my mom's health issue, I'm not looking for a sub right now." Heather immediately caught herself. Why did she make this offer? What did she want from Ted, and why?

She was so matter of fact about this, and Ted wasn't sure what to make of her. He did sense her personal power and knew he didn't want to get into a verbal confrontation with her. He had no illusions about a woman's place, realizing that females were just as competent, maybe more, than men, and he would never talk down to any female he knew.

"Well, Heather, perhaps you can run it by Steve, and if he's good with it, maybe I might fit into your odd family."

Heather called Steve and asked about moving Ted in. "Is he your boyfriend?"

"No, just a friend from school. Very nice. Probably not interested in making him my sub."

"Let me think about it and get back to you when you come down this weekend."

She let Ted know at their next class together, saying that thinking about it was pretty promising. Steve was the kind of guy who would usually make up his mind quickly, particularly about his house, so maybe it could happen.

When she arrived Friday afternoon, Lisa was

still looking weak and pale, but her doctor had said she was responding well to treatment, that the cancer was being beaten back, slowly, but still positive. Heather actually cried as she hugged her mom, telling her that she just knew a full recovery was imminent.

As usual, Lisa was in bed fairly early, and Heather got on her homework for an hour or so while Steve went through hundreds of emails, answering those that needed an answer, deleting the rest. Then by eleven, they retired to the living room for a glass of wine and conversation. "I've been thinking about your request, but that bedroom has been my guest room, and friends do come to stay now and then. However, the original owner had men's and women's locker rooms at the pool, and they are heated and have full bathrooms. If he can move a bed into one of them, and whatever furniture he needs, I can live with that."

Heather realized she'd never been in one of those bathhouses, that she trekked from pool to the house after drying off, so these places haven't been used for decades. She vowed to check them out the following week, and if suitable, she'd discuss it with Ted. She kind of liked the idea of having him in the house, but she wasn't sure why. She had decided not to want him as a sub, but she really enjoyed talking to him, and she thought he'd make a good addition to the group.

"Bathhouse, really?"

"Yeah, but as nice as any apartment you might have. The only thing that says bathhouse is the few lockers on one wall. The rooms are carpeted, two showers, take your pick, and toilets, sinks, places for your stuff. I think you might like it, so plan to come check it out after school."

He said he'd drop by that afternoon. Heather told Julie that Ted was coming over and let her know the boy was off limits. "Got it Heather. Your sub."

"No just a friend, but not a submissive guy at all. Like I said, a friend."

"Wow, Heather, I see what you mean. This is nice, heated, away from the main part of the house, privacy. It's a bit of a drive, farther than where I'm at now in Hidden Hills. I would like to thank him for the offer."

"You'll get your chance when he and mom come up next week. He has to give you his stamp of approval."

This was wonderful, Ted thought. He liked Heather, as a friend, or maybe a bit romantically, and he thought Steve Longwood was a cool actor. Being a nice guy actually pays off, he figured.

After seeing the room, Heather invited him to the main house to meet Julie. The first thing he noticed, since Julie was wearing a sleeveless shirt, was her muscular arms. Damn, he thought, her biceps look bigger than mine. This is an intimidating woman.

Julie brought him a glass of wine, informing him that since they were all underage, alcohol was not allowed, so if he was thinking he was drinking wine, he was obviously mistaken. She followed that up with a wink. "I hope you don't get in trouble with that beverage on your breath."

"No problem. By the time I get home the folks will be in their bedroom watching TV." Then curiosity got the better of him and he just had to ask. "You look like a bodybuilder. Are you?"

"Thank you for noticing, Ted. Yes, I'm working on that, but not ready yet to compete. Maybe next year. To tell the truth, my subs seem to get excited about my muscles. Do they excite you?" She caught Heather's disapproving look, and added that she was just kidding.

Ted, not picking up on the subtle exchange responded. "I think you look great, but muscles are neither a turn on or a turn off. I really don't think about stuff like that."

For some reason, one she couldn't pin down, Heather liked hearing that from him.

After he left, Julie, remembering what Heather had said, promised that she would totally leave him alone, particularly because she had gotten to the point where she was only interested in guys who admired her muscular body. It was part of her developing dominant personality.

Steve called Heather one weeknight. "About that boy you want to have move in, I'd like to meet him, and I'll be up there in a couple of days. Think you can have him come by?"

"I think so. He really likes the idea of living here."

"Good. I'll text you my itinerary."

The next day in biology class, Heather asked Ted

if he were free to meet with Steve on Thursday evening, and the idea of meeting a famous movie star was enough to have him say "Hell yes," thinking that anything else he might have to do could be put off.

Heather said to be there at seven thirty, and Ted made sure he was there exactly on time, not wanting to blow this chance to meet Steve and to get a really cool place to live rent free. "Hi mister Longwood. My name is Ted…"

Steve cut him off. "Call me Steve. Now Ted, tell me a bit about yourself."

Ted nervously started to tell him about his major, his plans for the future, his possible career, and then he said, "Please Mr., I mean Steve, don't worry about your daughter. We're just friends, and you know, I'm not going to well, you know."

Steve laughed. "I'm more worried about you Ted. Heather is, well, how should I put this, a man eater. If you're not careful, she'll have you on your knees."

"Yes sir. She told me about her dominant personality and all that, but she knows I'm not into that BDSM stuff, and she seems cool with that."

"You seem to be a nice kid, but if she gets too overpowering, just give me a call. She mostly listens to me, and I'll keep her from turning you into a domestic servant."

"Thank you sir, Steve, I've already promised to do my share of the chores, which is totally fine. I'm even cooking one night a week, and I hope to fix something that pleases the girls."

"Excellent. However, I'd be careful calling them girls. They consider that demeaning, and they won't put up with it from anyone but me and Heather's mom. Do you have a way to move your stuff here?"

"I can borrow my dad's truck, and I don't have much, bed, dresser and a big chair, plus my clothes and that sort of stuff."

"Then you don't need my help. Good. Lisa takes most of my time. I guess Heather has told you."

"Yes sir, I mean Steve. I have to say what a thrill it is to meet you. I've seen most of your movies."

"Then you've wasted a lot of time. Most of my films were action stuff, no depth, except that last three. If you haven't seen them, please do. Now, I have to have a chat with Heather."

Ted thanked Steve profusely and then left, not wanting to overstay his welcome. Then Steve called Heather in to his study. "Ted's a nice boy. I hope you aren't planning on turning him into your domestic slave."

"Dad, you won't believe this, but Ted is just a friend, the first male friend I've ever had. I wouldn't do anything to hurt him."

"Good. My little girl is growing up. I like that."

The following weekend Ted moved in. Heather was in Santa Monica with Lisa, but Julie was there, and she watched Ted wrestle with the big, overstuffed chair, half carrying, half dragging it, so she stepped in and offered to help. She picked it up, put it over her head and carried it into the pool house, while Ted stood there with his jaw dropped. Then she said, "Let's get the rest of your stuff." They carried in the bed and the dresser. Ted thought the dresser was heavy, but Julie looked like it was nothing at all. Within a few minutes they had everything moved in and Ted, somewhat intimidated, thanked her for the help.

"No problem new roomy. Now, perhaps you could return the favor by putting together some dinner for us."

Ted got busy, cooked, cleaned up after and then excused himself and went to his new room to study and to get away from Julie, who made him uncomfortable.

Monday afternoon, Heather, home from school after being away all weekend, found Ted pretty much settled in. "Sorry I wasn't here to help, but it looks like you got it all moved."

"Julie helped. In fact she carried that big chair in over her head. She is so strong."

Something about that hit Heather wrong, and it irritated her that he was in apparent awe of her friend. "Well, if you're so damn impressed with her muscles, maybe you should be her new submissive." Once said, she realized how it sounded, but it was too late to backtrack.

"No, Heather. I'm not a bit interested in being her submissive. I'm really not into muscular women." He remembered Steve's admonishment about calling them girls. "I just thought how amazing that she is so strong. It's not like anything I fantasize about."

Heather felt better hearing this, but she couldn't figure out why she should care one way or the other about his feelings for Julie. Perhaps she just wanted her friend all to herself, him being her first male friend. It was kind of a weird jealousy. She knew Julie well enough to know she wouldn't do anything about this, after the talk they'd had. After all, men come and go, but best friends are forever.

Still, she had to have confirmation. "So, no interest in Julie at all?"

"No, I'd rather, well, never mind."

"Rather what? "

"Not important. Never mind, really." He turned and walked out of the room, and Heather was thinking that maybe he was hinting to be her boy toy, but she knew he wasn't into being a submissive, so she decided to just let it go for now.

It actually worked out pretty well. Ted cooked Monday, Julie Tuesday and Heather Wednesday. Thursday they just got take out. Friday Heather headed from school straight down to Santa Monica to take care of Lisa. Steve had spent the night the day he met with Ted, having some business to take care of in Santa Barbara, nothing he was willing to share with Heather.

Chapter 19

Over a glass of Steve's wine, Heather mentioned how Ted was impressed with Julie's strength, and she had no idea why she'd brought it up. Ted was in his own room, apparently studying for an exam. Julie said, "I watched him struggle with that big chair, so I just grabbed it and carried it in. Being strong has its advantages. Did he make a big deal about it?"

Heather had to think about it for a minute. He really hadn't. He'd just commented on her physical strength, one short comment. It wasn't like he was getting all effusing about it. "No, I guess not. Just mentioned the chair thing. He doesn't look that weak, so he couldn't handle the chair?

"You know, when you lift, you learn how to get under something, get it up and over your head. I think he probably could have done it had he known how. He doesn't look too strong, but not a weakling either I'd guess."

"Maybe I'll see if he'll arm wrestle you." They both laughed, both knowing she would easily win.

When Heather arrived Friday, Lisa wasn't there, and Steve told her she'd gone to the hospital, some kind of complication.

"Why didn't you tell me? " Heather was getting angry.

"Just happened today. You were in class, and another hour or two wouldn't have made a difference. However, if you want to go, we can head there right now."

They jumped in Steve's car and headed to the hospital. Normally, Heather would love riding in his fast sport car, but this time she really wasn't paying attention, other than realizing she was glad he was driving, as she wasn't in a good place to be behind the wheel.

"Mom, what happened?"

"Got weak and passed out. Mister worry panicked and called 911. I'm really okay, trust me."

Steve said, "I'll always rather be safe than sorry."

That evening, Lisa still in the hospital for observation, Steve looking haggard and drawn, Heather poured him and herself a glass of wine. "You did the right thing dad. Like you said, better safe than sorry. Mom always acts like this fucking cancer is no big deal. If she were home, she'd try to fix us dinner."

"When did I stop being Steve and start being dad?"

Heather laughed, a cold, humorless laugh. "I guess you've always been dad, but I'm a big self-protective. My real dad was emotionally absent, totally, and it's taken me some time to trust. After all, when I met you, you were the dashing, babe magnet, movie star, and I was afraid you'd up and leave mom."

"And now?"

"You are a rock, dad, and I wish you had been my real, biological dad."

"Heather, you know you don't have to be here every moment you aren't in class. I can take care of your mom. There isn't really much you can do."

"I can show that I'm there for her, just like she's been there for me. I want her to know that she's my real mom, my mom, my friend, my confidant."

"You are an odd young woman, but the longer I know you, the more I care about you. Your odd sexuality and your odd history don't seem as, well odd, as I once thought. You were pretty mixed up, but it looks like you're finding your way."

"If so, I have you and mom to thank for that."

"If you don't mind me asking, what's with you and this Ted guy?"

"He's just a good friend from school, a guy I can talk to, someone who listens. Why do you ask?"

"I saw the way he looked at you, and well, he's definitely interested in you."

"No, he knows about my dominant nature, and he wants no part of it, so I don't think so."

"He may not want to be in that kind of relationship, but he certainly has a thing for you. Can't you see it?"

"Maybe I'm missing something, but no, I can't

see anything like that. Well, even if he is, I'm not changing who I am, and I don't see him changing who he is."

"People change. Take me for instance. When I met your mom I had a rule, never date a woman over thirty. That seems a lifetime ago."

Heather looked long and hard at Steve, now just dad, but once quite the playboy, and she had only heard bits and pieces, "so since we are here, mom in the hospital and wine in our hands, I'd like to hear more."

"Okay, if we have to go there." He took his glass and got comfortable on the couch. Heather sat, cross legged, across from him in a chair. "I really didn't have friends, lots of acquaintances and hanger-on types, wanting to be seen with a famous star, and the two or three almost friends used to call me Steve Shallow. I was arrested for hitting a rude guy in a bar, and that's when I met your mom. She was unimpressed, to put it mildly, but she helped me out of the mess, had me write an apology and pay his emergence room bill, and it all went away. I was impressed with her and invited her to lunch, not romantic at all. She was at least a decade too old by my standards. Well, we became friends, and that slowly changed to what we have now, and I wouldn't go back for the world. I'm not hungry any longer, no more longing for the next thrill. I'm a comfortable middle age man, and madly in love with your mom. Well, that sort of sums it up."

Heather smiled at his account. "So, before you met mom, you hit on only young women at bars?"

He sighed. "Guilty as charged."

"So had I been in a bar, you would have hit on me?"

"Probably. You were sort of my type."

"And I would have told you I was a dom, and you'd say?"

"Thanks, but no thanks. But it's all academic. You were and still are too young to get served in a bar.

"Actually Dad, I've been served in bars."

"I hope you don't carry a false ID."

"No, but this is fun. Let me tell you. I was on the way back from class, worried about a paper I had to write, worried about Mom, so I stopped in this bar, walked up all confident, sat down and nodded to the bartender. When he came over, I said, so very casually,

'I'll have my usual.' Well, that caught him off guard and he said he was sorry but he didn't remember me. I fixed him my best dom look, this one." She narrowed her eyes, fixed her jaw in a stern grin and just stared. "Well, I gave him this for like fifteen seconds, saw how uncomfortable he looked and then shrugged and said Black Label and soda. Well, he relaxed, made my drink and didn't even ask for my ID."

"I must say you have a way about you. I'm sure you wilt lots of guys with that look."

"Many of them, and the ones I can't wilt, I don't bother with. How about I refill your glass?"

They changed the subject, and Heather wanted to ask what he would do if they lost Lisa, but she couldn't bring herself to even think about it, let alone voice it to Steve, seeing how emotionally fragile he seemed.

The following day Heather cleaned the house, top to bottom. Steve had tried to keep it up, but it was obviously a man's limited concept of clean, so she went over everything. I'll have to tell mom to train him better, she thought.

Ted was waiting for her with a seat saved as usual. He smiled and asked her how her mom was doing.

"Trip to the ER, but looks like she'll be okay to come home today."

"You've told me so much about her, I would love to meet her one day."

That caught Heather by surprise, and she looked at him more closely than she had in the past. Was Steve right? Did this boy have a thing for her? She tried to read his face, but it just seemed the face of a good friend. She considered asking him point blank, but what if he answered in the affirmative? We'd be back to the I'm a dom, but you aren't a sub situation. What's the point, she thought. Instead, she tried a round about approach.

"Ted, do you have a girlfriend?"

He got a look that seemed anxious, like he was waiting for the next question, one he was obviously hoping to answer yes. "I don't have a girl friend. I mean, I date now and then, but no special girl." He emphasized "special," apparently an attempt to show that he wasn't desperate, but he had no close relation-ship. Perhaps, she thought, Steve might be right. He was looking at her, waiting for the next question, which she didn't have for him, so she just smiled and opened her notebook.

Finally, he could wait no longer, so he asked, "Why are you asking?"

"No special reason, just curious. I'm sure you just haven't found the right one yet."

There was a fleeting look in his eyes, disappointment, but he quickly recovered and smiled at her. "Yes, I guess not."

"I'm on probation at school." Julie announced at dinner one night. Both Heather and Ted looked at her, waiting for the rest of the story. "Academic?" Heather asked.

"No, it was about a fight."

Ted looked at her and asked. "You mean you were in a fight?"

"Duh, yeah. They wouldn't put me on probation for someone else's fight."

Heather took a breath. "Okay, so what happened?"

"I was in the student union, having a coffee, and this guy started talking to me. I really wasn't in the mood to chat, but you know how some clueless guys are. However, when he said I was a cute girl, I said, "wait just a minute. I'm eighteen, a grown woman, not a fucking girl."

He said, "Relax, babe. To me you are a girl, so just chill."

Then I said, "I'll give you one chance to apologize before I deck you."

He shook his head and said, "weird girl."

"So you hit him?"

"Laid him out on the floor, almost out cold. Security guard came over and asked what was wrong, and I said this guy insulted me."

"He helped the guy up and ask his side of the story, and the asshole said all I did was call her a girl. Of course the stupid guard couldn't see a problem, so I explained that calling a grown woman a girl is demeaning, and I won't stand for it. That's when he escorted us to some office where we had to make a statement."

Ted was sitting there with his mouth open in apparent disbelief. "That's one mistake I'm not going to make."

"I wouldn't hit a roommate, but glad I intimidate you."

Heather was observing her friend and the changes she'd been going through. "You seem to enjoy intimidating men. Not a bad thing, but an observation. Seems the more muscular you become, the more you enjoy it."

Julie, thinking about what Heather said, started flexing, not obviously, subtly, almost without thinking. "Yeah, I think you're right. The other day I caught some guy staring at me, so I walked over and asked him what he was looking at. He tried to say he wasn't looking, but I got in his face and called him a liar. Then he said he was admiring my muscles, and I said, "Good boy. You may go."

Ted was blown away. "So what did he do?"

"He thanked me and scuttled off like a good boy. I've been trying to get Heather to work out more, build some muscle. What do you think?"

Ted felt he was being put on the spot. "I don't know, being in good shape is important, but maybe big muscles isn't. I don't work out, but I guess I'm strong enough, so it's really hard to tell."

Julie was on a roll. "In my opinion, men shouldn't work out. Weak men are sexy and easy to dominate. Women should be stronger."

"Well," Ted said, "That is your opinion. I don't think many would agree with you."

Julie laughed. "Yeah, you are probably right, but in a perfect world..."

"Speaking of a perfect world, what's your mom's recovery looking like?" That was Ted trying to change the subject. Also, seeing that the women were out of wine, and trying to be the good new roommate, he hopped up, grabbed the bottle and refilled their glasses, plus a bit for himself, just to be sociable.

Heather was already in her pajamas, so that at some point when the late hour and the wine combined, she could just go into her room and drop into bed, flicking off the light as she dropped. Julie, on the other hand, seemed rather wound up and would probably study until late. Ted, more interested in hanging out with Heather, would likely excuse himself as soon as Heather went to bed. He really didn't want to spend much time with Julie. She was always nice to him, but there was something about her that made him feel like she was looking down on him, nothing he could put his fingers on, but just a feeling, one he couldn't either name or push out of his thoughts.

A couple of evenings later, Ted arrived after a late afternoon class to find Heather curled up in a plush living room chair, reading a book for class, Julie nowhere to be seen.

"Hi Heather. Looks like Julie isn't home."

Heather looked up from her book, gave him an appraising look and said, "No. I think she is with one of her subs. Are you disappointed that she's not home?"

That caught Ted by surprise. "Not at all. Just curious."

"So, honestly, if her muscular body turns you on, you should just admit it."

"No, not really. There's a certain fascination about a muscular woman, but I'm really not interested."

Heather put her book down and started to study him, making him a bit uncomfortable. Finally, she said, "Really? Not a bit?"

"There's always a bit of forbidden fruit kink, but I would never want to be involved with someone like that, not a bit. Why?"

"Just curious. Seems you don't have a girlfriend, at least none you talk about or bring around."

As much as he hated to admit it, he answered, "I don't have a girlfriend, not dating since my last girlfriend and I split up months ago. I guess I'm too busy at school to have time to go looking."

By now, Heather's book was on the table, a bookmark at the spot she was reading. She gave him that look again, one that he felt was looking straight into him, making him uncomfortable. She had this habit of just staring for the longest time before speaking, making him fidget, bring up his insecurities. Finally, she said, "Too bad. You're a nice guy and not too bad to look at. Probably lots of women on campus who'd go out with you."

He was tempted to ask if she were one of those, but knowing her sexual interests, he decided not to go there. Instead he thanked her, pulled out his school work and dropped into another of the plush chairs.

They both studied until ten, which was the agreed upon hour to relax with a glass of wine and some socializing. Ted, opened a bottle, reminding himself to find a way to replenish the supply, poured both of them a glass and sat down. The wine gave him the courage to ask a question. "You seem to have all those subs, but I never see one and you are here every night except when you're down south."

"Subs come and go, but my mom and my classes are high priority right now. I can always find a guy to play with, but now isn't the time."

He got a funny look, so she asked, "What?"

"The way you say play with, as if guys were just toys."

"Well, that's kind of how I see them, toys, playthings. I don't take any of them seriously."

That made him want to change the subject, so he asked about how she was doing on the biology assignment, and that led to a long discussion about DNA and inherited traits, which saved him from the subject of dating, sex and male toys.

Julie came in late, looking tired and disheveled. Said hello, asked how their evening went and went straight to her room.

"She looked beat," Ted noted.

"Yeah, all the play can tire one out."

Friday morning they all went to school, each with a different schedule, each in their own car. Heather and Ted had the same classes on Friday, but she left right after class for Santa Monica, so she didn't want to drive clear back to Montecito. In class that morning, a young woman started talking to Ted, acting interested, flirting actually, and for some reason it bothered Heather, and she wanted to make some excuse to interrupt, but then she thought better of it. Better Ted find someone to date, and better that she shouldn't get possessive since it couldn't go anywhere. Still, it bothered her until class was over and they went for coffee. She decided to ask, "That gal seems interested in you. What do you think of her?"

He shrugged. "I don't know. She's okay I guess."

Heather wasn't satisfied with that short answer, but she couldn't think of a way to push it further. Damn men, she thought, you have to drag any information out of them. Better to have them as subs so you don't have to bother with their opinions.

Heather had the ability to switch her focus totally, in this case from Ted to her mom, as she left the school parking lot and impatiently navigated through school traffic to the highway, hitting the button on the phone, which was on a holder on the dash, hands free as Lisa had drilled into her head. "Mom. I'm on the way home. How are you doing and do you need anything?"

Lisa assured her that she was fine and didn't need a thing except to chat with her lovely daughter.

Chapter 20

Heather had taken to wearing faded, lose-fitting jeans and an old sweatshirt, and this was almost every day. This had happened almost without forethought, just a default by someone who has stopped caring about her appearance. Showering and combing her hair were her attempts to stay neat looking. Friday traffic was a mess, whether on the freeway or on Highway One. It was an hour on a good day, but on a Friday afternoon, traffic could stop no matter which way she drove, and it was never easy. The freeway was longer, but with minimal traffic is was slightly quicker, but in Southern California, minimal traffic is something you discover by accident. Heather had elected Highway One, thinking that it would be just as fast, shorter and more interesting. However, an accident had brought traffic to a dead stop, and Heather was rapidly losing her temper.

When she saw people getting out of their cars, walking around, chatting, looking out at the beach, she realized there was a serious problem. She called Lisa, but there was no answer, so she called Steve, and it rang several times before he answered. "I'm stuck behind some major accident, and I don't know how long this will be. I called mom, but no answer."

There was an uncomfortable silence for what seemed a long time, but was probably just seconds. "She's back in the hospital. I don't know anything yet, and by the way, you aren't going anywhere for a long time. There's a fuel tanker on it's side in Malibu, and gasoline all over the road. Take Mulholland if it's close enough."

She pulled up the map app to check and saw that Mulholland was a windy road that would take fucking forever, but from what Steve was saying, she'd be stuck here for fucking forever. Well at least on Mulholland, she would be moving, growing closer to home, closer to seeing her mom and finding out why she was in the hospital, so remembering that she'd just passed the turnoff, she made a U turn and drove back to the junction, and apparently many others had the same idea. As she crawled up the narrow, winding road, following a long line of cars, she was getting more and more angry and impatient. She remembered a meditation CD in her glove box, one Lisa had given her, one she hadn't bother listening to, so she pulled it out, pushed it in the player and tried to focus.

    It was soft music and some commentary, and as she listened to the guy saying that things happen, but what matters is how you react to them, that circumstances are what they are, but your reaction determines if they are bad or not. Fuck yes, she thought. I can't do a thing about this, so best relax and enjoy the scenery. Soon she was focusing on the beauty of the Santa Monica Mountains, wondering why she'd never been up this road before, realizing how much of life is missed when you are in a hurry. She then had a minor epiphany. All this wasn't about mom as much as it was about her. There wasn't a thing she could do for Lisa, but her own feeling of importance told her she had to be there, had to be the one at the center of it all. She thought about Mom fighting for her life and selfish Heather thinking about herself. I can do better, she thought. I can love her without being the drama queen. I can do what needs to be done without making it about me.

    The normally just over an hour trip ended up taking better than four hours, and she didn't arrive until almost nine at night, too late for visitor hours at the hospital, but she realized that there wasn't a damn thing she could do about it except hug and comfort Steve and keep him company.

    "Honest opinion dad. Do I act like a self-centered drama queen?"

    "Honest opinion, sometimes, but I understand why, and it isn't all the time, so it's cool."

    "I'm trying to do better."

    "You are eighteen, in the process of maturing, so you're not expected to be perfect yet. Hell, I have almost three decades on you, and I'm not perfect yet, despite what my fans think." He smiled at the irony.

In a moment of introspection, Heather concluded, "You know that you and Ted are the first two men I've liked at all, tolerated actually. I guess that's maturity or a start anyway."

Steve's smile started to give way to a deep belly laugh. "I guess that's as close to a compliment I'm likely to get. It's always good to be tolerated."

Realizing what she'd said, Heather backtracked. "Perhaps tolerate isn't the right word. I've passed that and gotten all the way to like. In your case, Dad, it boarders on love, but don't get all sappy on me."

Finally, Heather got up to go to bed. "Dad, let's get to the hospital the minute visiting hours start. I can't wait to see Mom."

They were at the hospital first thing in the morning, having to wait a few minutes for visiting hours to officially begin. Heather rushed to Lisa's room and saw a pale, gaunt woman with sunken eyes. "What happened mom?"

"Just weak. Couldn't stand up, so called 911, and they brought me here. Doctors said it was the chemo and radiation really knocking me on my ass."

"Oh no. What are they saying about your condition? I hope it isn't getting worse."

"Actually, all this bad stuff is kicking ass on my cancer. I'm improving, if I can stand the cure."

Just then a doctor walked in and asked Lisa if she were ready to go home.

Heather spoke up, asking if it was safe and what was really going on, her natural instinct is to not trust damn near anyone except her mom, dad and close friends.

The doctor, a woman in her mid forties, smiled and tried to reassure Heather. "The treatments were making her weak, so we kept her overnight for observation. Obviously she's a long way from cured, but she's good to go home. Just have her keep quiet, relaxed, no making big meals, cleaning the house, cutting the lawn. Stuff like that."

"Rest and relaxation?"

"Exactly. Now let's all move out of the room and let the nurse help her get dressed."

Back at the house, Heather went to work in the

kitchen, fixing a meal that was light but nutritious. Lisa could only eat a small portion, the meds ruining her appetite.

"You said the meds were pushing the cancer back. Does that mean you are getting well?"

"It means I'm headed in the right direction. According to the oncologist, the prognosis is good, and I'm very likely to get well. I'm almost, sort of out of the woods."

Heather was hoping for two thumbs up, bye bye cancer, hello the good life, but what Lisa was saying was far better than nothing, so Heather tried to hide her apprehension.

Lisa was taking a moment to phrase her next question, knowing how defensive Heather can be, but she managed to settle on the words she wanted. "So, this boy, Ted, who is living with all of you, what's that all about."

Heather got the implied question. "Mom, he's just a friend. We have a biology class together, go for coffee after class, talk about stuff. He's nice, but, well, you know, he's not into being a sub, so just friends."

Lisa was studying Heather's face as she spoke. Then she let a slight smile appear for a moment before saying, "Okay, I see, a nice new friend."

Heather wanted to say more, but defending something left unsaid was the same as admitting mom's suspicions, so Heather let it drop.

Steve said, "If Lisa is up to it, we're going downtown tomorrow for lunch. Want to join us?"

"I would love that."

School was closing for the Christmas holidays, and Heather had no reason to stay in Montecito, although Julie decided to hang out there, being that she wasn't anxious to stay in her old childhood bedroom and that she had her subs all scheduled neatly for her enjoyment. Ted would also stay there, and Julie knew that to start anything with him would be to lose Heather's friendship, which was far more important than one more sub.

Nadia was also going to drive up for a few days, kind of settle in for the upcoming semester, after her January graduation. Julie made it clear to Nadia that absolutely no alcohol, not a drop. "I don't want to be responsible for you falling off the wagon."

She did assure her that there were plenty of potential subs at college, and that she would have all she had time for, reminding her that college classes were harder than those in high school.

In order not to tempt Nadia, Julie didn't have any wine while Nadia was around, and Ted, who only drank with the women to be sociable, was more than happy to skip the nightly wine.

When Nadia met Ted, she looked him over carefully and took Julie aside. "I want him, but if he's yours or Heather's I won't act on it."

"He's sort of Heather's, but it's weird. He's not her sub, but she's jealous for some reason I can't figure out. Either way, it's best to leave him alone."

"Too bad. I was fantasizing about him licking my feet before I pegged him. The idea makes me so damn horny. Funny, now that I can't drink, sex is even more important."

What was it about the women in this house than made Ted so uncomfortable. The new gal, Nadia, still in high school, looked at him like a hungry cat at a bird, and it spooked him. Like most men, Ted felt more comfortable being the one to make the first move, the woman either giving him a positive or negative response. These gals were very aggressive to the point of acting like predators. So here was this girl, right, still a girl for a few more months, almost three years younger, making him feel like a shy little boy. Well, he and Heather were friends, maybe, hopefully, a bit more, and this was a very cool place to live, so he would try to get along with both Julie and Nadia. He was glad the obligatory wine hour was retired.

Curled up in one of the overstuffed chairs in the spacious living room, Ted was studying and taking notes when Nadia walked in and sat down near him. "What's up Ted?"

"Just studying for a test. I'm a sophomore and each year the work load gets bigger. Enjoy high school while you can."

"Yeah, both Julie and Heather warned me about college, but I actually like to study. So what are you majoring in?"

"Biology. I think I'd like to do some work in genetics."

"Me too. We actually got to sequence some DNA

in my biology class, and I thought it was fun."

Suddenly predator was turning into potential friend, someone with the same interests. "You know there are still parts of the genome that they can't figure out what it's for."

"I think it's probably junk DNA or that stuff that turns other DNA on or off."

"Yeah, I think you're right. I can tell you which professors are interesting and which are boring or too hard."

"I'd appreciate that. Heather has herself a keeper in you."

"Heather and I, well, there is no Heather and I. Just friends."

"Oh yeah. Sure."

She obviously didn't believe it. What was it with them, assuming he and Heather had some relationship. Did she say something to them, something she neglected to tell him. Well, it didn't matter, as he knew what kind of relationships she had with men, and while he liked strong women leaders, all that kinky stuff was a non starter.

However, since Nadia wasn't allowed to drink and Ted didn't particularly care for it, they spent those late hours after study time talking about biology, a mutual interest, and they started becoming friends. He was surprised that a girl her age already had a history of being a dominatrix, but it wasn't a subject he even wanted to discuss with her. Best, he thought, too keep it about biology, DNA and nothing personal. In fact, he even offered to help her move as soon as she graduated, which was soon.

Chapter 21

With a break between semesters, Heather stayed in Santa Monica, calling Julie occasionally just to check in and make sure Steve's house was still fine. The idea of doing any damage to Dad's place wasn't even something she would consider.

Lisa was home, getting stronger, actually putting on a bit of weight after getting so thin she looked like a stiff breeze would blow her away. Color was coming back to her cheeks, and Heather finally started thinking that Mom would survive and heal. So, during the break, Heather became chef, nurse, comforter and house cleaner.

"Heather dear, you are spoiling me. Relax. I can do more now, and you don't need to beat yourself up."

"In a few more days I'll be back in school, so please let me spoil you for these few days." Heather was standing there in a pair of faded jeans, hair pulled back into a pony tail and a tattered sweatshirt.

Steve was also there, and he was anxious to help spoil Lisa, but every time he found something to do, Heather was already on it. The girl seemed to be everywhere at once.

Lisa's phone rang, and when she picked it up, she let out a yelp. "Oncologist called. Cancer is in full retreat, almost gone, and I can hopefully stop taking this powerful poison very soon."

"We will go out tonight to celebrate," Steve decreed.

Heather made a quick call to Julie. "Mom is getting well."

Lisa was enjoying a cocktail, first one she had been able to drink in months. Heather was watching her, afraid of some possible reaction, but Steve was relaxed and enjoying himself. Lisa looked at Heather who was looking at her and said, "I'm much better dear. You don't have to spend every weekend with me, as much as I appreciate it and enjoy your delightful company."

Heather thought about it for a moment, thinking about the horrid traffic on Friday afternoons, and then she proposed a compromise. "How about I come up Saturday and leave Sunday evening?"

"You mean, every weekend?"

"Of course."

"I guess that will do for now, but as I improve, you need to make more Heather time. Okay?"

"Deal, mom."

The following Friday Heather realized that she didn't have to bolt after her last class and fight the traffic, and she mentioned it to Ted during class. Ted came up with an idea but wrestled with it for some time before getting up the nerve to say something. "Instead of cooking, perhaps we could go out someplace in Santa Barbara, sort of celebrate your mom's improvement."

Heather looked at him and realized that the last time she'd been on an actual date, not playing with a sub, was when she killed that guy with his own knife. That seemed so long ago. She tried to remember how it felt to be that angry fourteen year old girl, but it didn't seem to be her any longer. Males used to make her angry, but now she regarded them as something like a hobby. However, Ted was looking at her expectantly, and she figured, what the hell. Let's see what a date feels like. "Sure, have a place in mind?"

"How about the Boathouse, right on the water, great views and very..." He almost said romantic but caught himself in time. That would have been a deal killer.

"Very what." She wanted him to finish the sentence.

"Very easy to find and plenty of parking. Besides the food is good."

"Sounds great, and it's close to home. Since it's on the way home, let's take both cars, so we don't have to drive back to school."

He agreed, although he would have loved to drive her there like a real date. They agreed on a time to meet, and he called to make a reservation and was strangely uneasy the rest of the day. Women didn't usually intimidate him, but she managed. Her matter of fact talking about her subs and how she played with them was very unsettling, but somehow fascinating.

Ted arrived a few minutes early, secured the table and waited patiently for Heather, who arrived just a few minutes late without commenting on her punctuality. Ted wasn't going to blow it by saying anything, so being that neither of them were old enough to drink and Ted looked two or three years younger than his twenty years, they opted for ice tea. Ted reminded her that this was his treat, so Heather ordered the lobster, which made him think about how much money he had. Well, there goes my plans for the weekend, he thought. He asked her how she liked the place, and she said it was charming, the food was good, and she was impressed.

Ted couldn't understand why he was so damn happy to hear this or why he was so anxious to impress this girl who he could never have a real relationship with. Still, they enjoyed the meal, and since it wasn't night yet, they took a twilight walk along the beach, him thinking how he'd like to hold her hand but knew that wouldn't work.

When they got to their cars, she thanked him for a lovely evening and that she'd see him at home. On the drive home, she thought about whether she felt anything either sexual or romantic about him and their lovely evening, and she decided she felt nothing either way.

Julie was out, and Nadia hadn't moved in yet, so Heather and Ted had a glass of some of Steve's finest and then she said that she wanted to get a very early start in the morning, to get to Santa Monica before weekend traffic started up, so she thanked him for the evening and said goodnight.

The following morning, Heather arrived early, sun hovering over the ocean, reminding her that the California didn't go north to south, but east to west, to find Steve and Lisa having an animated conversation. "So, you're telling me that Megan doesn't even know you've been sick? She's a close friend."

"I don't need any more people hovering over me like I'm about to drop dead."

"She should know. Tomorrow, we should go to My Goodness for breakfast, let her know you've been sick and are getting better."

Heather hadn't seen Megan for months, nor had she been to My Goodness for breakfast, and she really liked Megan, so as she entered the room she announced, "I vote for My Goodness. I like Megan and I miss her."

Lisa shrugged, indicating she'd been outvoted, so in the morning they headed downtown to the little hole in the wall restaurant that Lisa actually owned a share in, and found Megan waiting tables, her new, female, cook in the back. "Shit, look you just wandered in. Been months. What's up with you girlfriend and Steve, and wow, Heather's all grown up."

"Give me a break Megan, it's only been like four months since I've been here, and by the way, place looks great. New paint job?"

Then Megan took a closer look at Lisa and saw that something was wrong. "Girlfriend, you don't look well. What's up?"

"Just a bit of cancer. I'm getting better. No problem."

"A bit of cancer, no problem? I'm not buying that. Come on.

"Okay. Breast cancer, mastectomy, chemo, radiation, cancer is shrinking, and it's almost gone. End of story."

"End of story? I don't fuckin think so. Look, I'm your friend, and I'm here to help you, so don't be all noble about this and just let me in."

Steve, who was quiet up to then, had to speak up. "I agree with Megan. You need all the friends you can get while you continue fighting this. Don't confuse stubbornness with strength."

Heather reluctantly said she agreed with both of them, and Lisa, outnumbered, bowed to their wisdom. "Okay, you can all treat me like a fragile invalid if it makes you happy."

Heather trusted Megan and her long friendship and business partnership with mom, so she was pleased to know there was one more person looking after her. Still, the breakfast was great as usual, the reason there were now three My Goodness restaurants in the area.

After breakfast, with the beach only two blocks away, Steve suggested taking a walk. Under a slightly overcast sky, the wind turning the ocean into multicolored chop, the sound of breaking waves on the sand, the cry of gulls circling overhead, and it was just as Heather had remembered it, living with Mom, walking to the beach and unfortunately thoughts of the two guys who had died there at her hands. She wasn't that way any longer. She was a woman who cared for her males, took care of them, emotionally protected them, even nurtured them. In return they did what their deep nature required of them, they obeyed and worshiped her.

People they passed on the beach often looked over, seeming to recognize Steve, but not being really sure. He looked the same, but his hair was going grey, his waist had expanded just a bit, and he dressed in sweats rather than designer jeans and all that expensive stuff. Heather could almost hear them, "Isn't that the actor, you know, action guy, Steve something."

"Naw, what would a guy like that be doing here." As if movie stars weren't real people with real lives and real families, guys who took walks with their families.

She had the urge to stop some of those people and say, "That's Steve Longwood, good actor and even better husband and father." But, she would never do that, never share him with strangers.

Lisa was feeling better, and instead of a short walk, they continued down to Pacific Palisades, all the way to Will Rogers State Beach. Looking up at the sandy bluffs, Heather could picture that first guy, what was his name, who she pushed off the edge. It was right about there, she looked up, remembering the yelp he gave out as he fell, thinking about her casual walk to the stairs and down to find him lifeless, remembering the sexual thrill, finding that now there was only sadness, no thrill. You've come a long way girl, she thought to herself.

Lisa looked over at her, seeing Heather lost in thought and looking up at the bluff. "That's where it happened?"

"Yeah Mom. It seems a lifetime ago. Hard to believe I'm the same person."

"Yes, my darling girl, I know."

By the time they got back it was clear that they'd overdone it. Lisa was exhausted and had to lay down. Heather and Steve had some coffee and chatted in the living room.

"We shouldn't have let her talk us into a long walk."

Steve shook his head. "On the contrary, that walk did her a load of good, pushed her, made her feel she was recovering. I know how much you care, but she had to push herself to improve, to get stronger. Being weak and helpless would bother her even more than the cancer. Any woman strong enough to tame a guy like me isn't going to let some silly cancer get the best of her."

Heather shrugged, acknowledging that he was right. Indeed, Mom was the strongest women she knew, someone who could put bad guys in jail and come home to fix a broken teen.

"I'm thinking about staying the night and getting an early start in the morning, before dawn, before traffic, before Mom wakes up."

"Fine, just make sure you make your first class. You are part of a family of college grads, so you have the responsibility to keep the tradition and hopefully pass it along to your kids."

"I don't see me having kids. I mean, I wouldn't do it alone, and I can't see me in a permanent relationship with some man."

"There was this thirty year old movie star who thought he had it all, all the women he wanted, fame, fortune, all that crap. If someone would have told him that he would end up in a relationship with a woman his age and have an adopted daughter, he would have laughed. So, never say never."

Heather muttered, "Yeah, I guess anything is possible. Ever miss your old life?" "Not really. I was surrounded by people, mostly those who wanted to be connected to a star, to gain something personal or financial from associating with me. Also, I acted like such an asshole, real people wanted nothing to do with me. Hollywood makes it sound so glamorous, but it's mostly smoke and mirrors."

Chapter 22

Ted was walking on a path on campus with one of his friends, and for some reason he had to remark. "I met this girl."

The friend, tall and thin, stopped and turned to him. "Sounds good. Got a relationship going with her?"

"Not exactly. I'm rooming with her and her friends in a big place in Montecito, and we did go on one sort of date."

"So, tell me more. Are you sleeping with her?"

"No. See, she's into being a dominatrix, and she has guys who are her subs, who obey her orders, kiss her feet and all that kinky stuff."

"That sounds like fun. Are you going to be her sub?"

"That doesn't appeal to me at all, even though I wouldn't mind having a woman who takes charge, like in bed and decisions about where we eat and stuff like that."

"Well, the idea of being a sub for some babe is pretty exciting. If you don't want to do it, introduce us."

The idea bothered him, even though he knew Heather would not want what BDSM people call a vanilla relationship, so they were relegated to just friends. Still, the idea of her being with this guy bothered the hell out of him. "I don't know. She's pretty busy with her sick mom, so she's put all that on hold for a time." That, he felt, was an easy out. He'd never suspected that so many guys would like being submissive to a dominant woman. Obviously Heather had no problem finding them, getting tired of one and landing another with apparent ease. As they walked on, Ted looked at the guys passing by, wondering if he could tell which were submissive, but he drew a blank.

That night he decided to ask. Both Heather and Julie were home, so he just blurted it out. "I notice that you two have no problem finding submissive men. Are they all that common?"

Julie laughed. "Dear boy, they are all over, coming out of the woodwork, begging to belong to a dominant woman."

Heather nodded and said, "I agree, sometimes I would talk to some guy, mention I was a dominant, and they would say something like they'd fantasized about it but hadn't tried it. Easy pickings."

"Yeah," Julie said. "Then I'd lean over and whisper in the guy's ear all the things I like my subs to do for me, and they were practically drooling. Males are so fucking easy."

"Yeah Ted," Heather said. "Sometimes I think you are more the exception than the rule."

Ted's mind was reeling. "I need a glass of wine. Anyone else?"

He got up found the open bottle and poured for each of them, and it felt somehow natural to serve them.

A week later Nadia moved in, just in time to start a new semester, and now the evenings involved three assertive doms and Ted, and he felt badly outnumbered. In the middle of the first week of the new semester, the four of them were sitting in the living room, each in a big, comfortable chair, each with homework to study or to do, but then, as it approached bedtime, the conversation started up, the three females discussing first their classes, and then their subs, of which Heather didn't currently have. Ted sat quietly, listening but not participating, feeling and probably looking quite uncomfortable. Nadia noticed it and said, "Are we intimidating you, Ted."

He had to admit it, feeling sheepish.

"Good," Nadia said. "We need to remind you of women's natural superiority. Men need to learn their place." With that she laughed, as if she were kidding, but Ted knew she was more serious than she let on.

Ted was trying to imagine how guys would like someone like her, a real ball buster.

Heather came to his defense. "Nadia, be nice to

Ted. He is part of our family, just as you are, so chill."

Nadia made a half assed apology and moved on to another subject. The evenings were no longer accompanied by wine, all having agreed that it wouldn't be fair to Nadia, a member of Alcoholics Anonymous and still seventeen. Actually Ted was glad, as wine tends to loosen inhibitions, and these three seemed to have few inhibitions even without any wine.

Julie was teasing Ted, saying how nice it would be if he wore sexy panties around the house, an idea he nixed immediately.

Ted and Heather still sat together in class, this time the next level biology class, and they still went for coffee after. He was helping her with an assignment over coffee, carefully explaining the concepts, showing her how to proceed. She looked at him, smiled and gave him a big hug. "My very first guy friend. Thank you for being you."

That short statement ran through his mind, over and over for the rest of the day, and he kept wishing that she wasn't a dominant, but rather a regular woman, not realizing that she considered herself a regular woman, but the non dominant were somehow odd women.

Ted was getting used to Nadia and her teasing, and he was no longer intimidated, but was starting to come up with cleaver rejoinders, keeping her just enough off balance to create domestic harmony. Life was settling down in the big Montecito house, and Steve was coming up less often, and then only when Lisa was up to it.

Lisa was improving, the cancer shrinking, her strength starting to come back, so she was coming to Montecito occasionally with Steve, as she was still on medical leave and couldn't go back to work, even though she could hardly wait to get back.

One evening when all six of them were in the house together, realizing that even six people in a house that big didn't feel at all crowded, Ted and Nadia finally became more intimately acquainted with Steve and Lisa. Steve using the charm he'd developed as a film actor, turned Nadia into a fan, and was becoming somewhat of a hero to Ted.

All of them decided to hit the pool one afternoon, but Lisa, uncomfortable with her mastectomy, wouldn't get into a bathing suit. Julie in a very skimpy bikini was obviously the most buff of the group, and even Steve, usually not someone to comment, had to praise her. "You are a serious bodybuilder, and you look great."

In response, Julie flexed, showing biceps that put the rest of them to shame.

Lisa wore a surfing rash guard, a semi wetsuit top which covered her lack of breasts, and while Heather wanted to say that none of them had a problem with her condition, she knew mom had a problem, and, rational or not, she respected that and kept quiet.

Later, sitting by the fire, Heather asked Lisa if she felt uncomfortable naked in bed. "Actually, I don't get naked in bed. I keep a tee shirt on. No body sees me naked any more."

"Hopefully you'll get over that. You are loved, boobs or not, so don't let that define you."

"Nice bit of wisdom, but it doesn't help. You can't imagine having scars where there were once breasts."

Now that Lisa was getting better, she and Steve came up to Montecito more often, enjoying it while they can since Lisa would soon be well enough to go back to work after months of recovery. Then the day came when she got the news. Cancer free, gone, not a trace.

Heather dropped everything and rushed to Santa Monica to celebrate with her mom. It was champagne, caviar, music and a lovely dinner, cooked by Heather and Steve. Even Julie came down for that, leaving Ted and Nadia in Montecito, both feeling like they were not close enough to take part. However, when they didn't come, Steve called and said they were very welcome and they should come down right away.

Megan and D'Wanda, Lisa's friends and business partners in My Goodness, were there. This was a tight-knit group, a made up family of diverse people, diverse but united by mutual respect.

"Heather, you don't need to come down every weekend now. I'm good and am going back to work, so enjoy being a single college student. Go play. Have fun."

Easier said than done. Heather had made being there for Lisa a high priority, all encompassing dedication, and now she will have to back off, perhaps go back to playing with subs, if those subs were still around. If not, finding new ones wouldn't be very hard.

One day over coffee with Ted, he suddenly blurted out, "Do you like to watch birds?"

Heather was taken by surprise and had to think for a few seconds. "Yeah, I guess that's pretty interesting. Why?"

"The Ventura River estuary, out past the pier is full of shore birds. Really interesting and cool. I'm thinking about going after my last class. Care to come along?"

Heather shrugged. "Sure, why not. I'm out of class by four."

They drove out past the pier, past the surfers, to the end of the road, parked and walked along the beach to the estuary. Grebes, gulls, pelicans and a few egrets swarmed the area, and Heather pulled out her phone and started to take pictures. "Wow, birds every fucking place out here. You were right."

They hung out until the sun started to sink, and then got back in the car and drove to Montecito, stopping at a diner for a quick meal, one Ted insisted on paying for.

That night, Nadia and Julie not being around, Heather and Ted enjoyed a glass of Steve's expensive wine and chatted about the day. "Thanks for taking me there. That was quite interesting."

Ted took a sip, spun it around in his glass and said, "We're getting spoiled. No way in hell we'll be able to afford this stuff when we are out and on our own."

"Steve has like maybe a hundred bottles in his wine cellar, and we just need to leave him enough for him and his guests. Without Nadia's help, we can make a bottle last two or three nights."

"I'll drink to that." As he sipped and looked over at Heather, Ted was feeling mellow and content. This girl was starting to get to him, and he knew he shouldn't let that happen, knew what she wanted in a relationship, something alien to him. This was forbidden fruit, and he was drawn to her despite the warnings in his head.

Heather was crawling into bed when she heard Julie come in. Midnight. Hope she can keep it together in her classes. Can't party nightly and still keep those grades up. But, what the fuck, Julie will keep it together or not, and she's too thick headed to be lectured to.

Over coffee in the morning, Heather in a robe, Julie in sweats, "have fun last night?"

"Yeah. I had two guys worshiping me. I made them kiss my bicep and call me Goddess. It was fun. Guys really love to be dominated. You need to get back in the game."

"Now that Mom is healthy again, I guess I should. Got to find a new submissive."

"You can borrow one of mine. Hell, It will be a gift to my best friend."

"Do I get to choose?"

"Sure, except for Alex. I'm enjoying training him."

Julie sent text messages to three of her subs, telling them to come over that evening. The idea was to have them there for Heather to inspect and to possibly pick one.

Being the obedient subs and anxious for whatever exciting activities Julie had planned for them, they arrived on time and anxious to find out what Julie had in mind. They were a bit freaked out seeing that they were all there.

"I guess you wonder why you were called here tonight. Well, my friend Heather needs a new sub, and I'm thinking about giving her one of you. Do any of you have a problem with Heather?"

Heather was wearing shorts and a halter top, and she was looking very sexy. One of the guys said he was so spoiled on muscular women that he wasn't interested in Heather, a normal sized woman. The other two had no problem at all. That's when Julie ordered them to strip for Heather's inspection. They were a bit uncomfortable at first, but the idea of being inspected by her, while standing there naked, was almost too much for them to imagine, so they dropped their pants and took off their shirts.

Heather was getting into this, and she walked back and forth in front of them, stroking each cock, watching them get hard and so excited they were almost ready to cum. Finally, Heather pointed to a slender, tall, blond guy and said, "I'll take this one."

Julie put her hand on the guy's shoulder and said, "You belong to Heather now, and I will be very disappointed if she is unhappy with you."

Heather looked at him, seeing how excited he was and said, "I need to see your submission. Get on your knees and kiss my feet."

He dropped to his knees and started kissing her feet, while she smiled at Julie and said, "Yes, he will do just fine. Thank you for the lovely gift."

Later, when in Heather's bed, the boy, Dave, while busy giving Heather head, her oddly thinking about Ted, imagining him between her legs, and the thought made her climax.

The following day over coffee, Heather decided to ask a personal question. "When you have a girlfriend, so you enjoy giving her oral sex?"

"Wow, that's out of the blue, but yes, I do enjoy it. I like to give any woman I'm with pleasure. Was this just academic or are you hinting about something?"

"Just curious, but is that something you'd like to do with me?"

"Well, I guess, if we were dating, but I guess we're not going to be doing that."

"Yeah, vanilla dating doesn't really do it for me."

Ted had heard the term vanilla before, referring to non-kinky relationships, and he chose to not pursue that conversation, switching to something more comfortable, like their biology class. "I guess we're going to do some stuff with DNA next week."

Heather, sensing his discomfort, followed him to the more comfortable subject. "I think that will be very interesting. Do you want to be lab partners?"

Ted lit up. "Yes, I think I'd like being your lab partner. We're good at helping each other."

Heather wanted to say she'd like to help herself to him, but she knew better than to go there.

Chapter 23

Steve's coming and going in Montecito was usually predictable, but one evening he came storming in, slamming the door behind him. The girls were in the living room, studying, Ted in his room. Steve called to Heather, asking her to come with him. They went into his room, and he pointed to a seat, which Heather took, getting concerned, thinking that perhaps Mom had a relapse. "Something's wrong? What's going on?"

"Lisa is upset, thinks I'm not attracted to her because of the mastectomy. She doesn't understand, and I don't know how to explain."

"Slow down dad. Start at the beginning."

"We were in bed, and she was feeling well romantic, and I just couldn't do it. She thinks it's because her missing breasts are a turnoff for me, which isn't the case at all."

"Than why weren't you able to have sex with her? It sort of sounds like she was right."

"It's that I feel, I don't know, sad for her, and that gets in the way of passion. You know, she seems so fragile, so broken, not the powerhouse she's always been, and I feel sorry for her. Yes that's it, sorry for her, and that gets in the way of sexual excitement. Does that make sense?"

Heather was sitting, but Steve was pacing back and forth between the bed and Heather. She was trying to pull her thoughts together, trying to find out what to say, trying to understand what Steve was feeling. Then she realized that she too had different feelings about her mom. The former pillar of strength had become someone who needed care, and that put her in a different light. "I understand, Steve. She's weak and vulnerable, not the take charge woman we are used to.

Maybe I could talk to her. Perhaps without the sexual dynamic, we could talk it out."

"Heather, that would be wonderful. I love that woman, and I can't imagine her believing that I no longer desire her."

"You do still desire her, right?"

He stopped pacing, pausing a moment to be sure of his feelings. "Yes, I still desire her, but things have become complicated, lots of issues all mixed up. I'm not sure I understand everything I'm feeling. She needs to know that."

"Trust me, Steve. I'll straighten it all out. That's just a partial repayment for all you've done for me and the girls."

Then she saw something she never imagined she would see, Steve crying, like a dam had burst, and she was not sure how to comfort him, but basic instincts took over, and she jumped up, wrapped her arms around him and held him close until the sobs abated.

Heather headed home Friday afternoon, anxious to talk to Lisa, but anxious about how to proceed. How do we discuss something as intimate as his inability to have sex with her, and his reasons why, which may or may not resonate with Lisa.

Mom, I saw something I'd never seen before, Steve crying like a baby. Looks like something pretty heavy has gone down around here."

"I'd say so. Apparently no boobs, no sex. I'm so fucking disappointed in that man."

"Mom, I don't think it's about that. He said he was feeling sad and sorry for you, with all the cancer, chemo and all that, and that got in the way of sex."

"Well, Heather, pity is only slightly better than disgust. Either way I'm not likely to want him in my bed again."

Heather started to see her family coming apart, reminding her of her original family and the way it fell apart, and she didn't want to go through that again. "Mom, guys are, well, just guys, and they try but screw up all the time. Please give it some time, and I think he'll adjust. I know he really loves you."

"Platonic love doesn't cut it Heather. The man I married is not the man who turned me down the other night."

"Well, even women get put out of the mood now

and then. I'll make sure he stays in Montecito until he's ready to deal with all this. Please, Mom, don't give up on him yet."

"Yeah, keep him in Montecito. He can call me when or if he gets his head together. In the mean time, he has his home, and I have mine."

Heather lie awake that night, staring at the ceiling, trying to sleep, trying to figure out how to make things right for her mom. Somehow this had morphed into her problem, her need to fix it, her need to prove she wasn't a jinx on other people's relationship, which was, and for reasons she couldn't define, how she was feeling at the moment. How would she explain all this to Steve. Men seem to lack the capacity for nuance.

In the morning, Lisa saw that Heather was distressed. "Honey, this isn't your problem. You don't need to fix anything for me."

"At least I can talk to Steve, find out what he's thinking."

Lisa shook her head, knowing that Heather wouldn't let this go. "Do what you must, but without my blessing. As much as I love you, don't expect me to get involved."

When Heather arrived in Montecito, Julie and Nadia were in their rooms, and Steve was in the living room with a very strong-looking drink in his hand, watching some nature show on TV. "Hi sweetie. How's your mom?"

Not wanting to sugarcoat it, Heather sat down opposite him and slowly said, "She's pretty angry right now."

Steve just shook his head and didn't say anything for a long time. Finally, with a deep sigh, "So, what do I do about this? You know I love her."

"And she loves you, but this is hard for her. You don't understand about women and their breasts. I mean, it's like you losing your balls or something like that."

"Yeah, and I'd give them up to fix this if I could."

"Do you want advice from some dumb kid."

"Absolutely, but you're anything but a dumb kid."

"Work this out for yourself, and when you are ready and your head is on straight, call her up and be contrite as all hell. Tell her how wrong you were. Being wrong works pretty well."

"You women don't think very highly of men do you?"

"You guys are good for dinner companions and sex, perhaps chores around the house, but not much more. "

"Stud service. That was me before I met your mom."

"Yeah, you were a hunk. Still are really. But relationships are different, but what do I know. I don't have relationships, just kinky sex with guys I don't give a flying fuck about."

"I know, and I think you're missing something. You get what you want, but you lose something perhaps important. You're young. Perhaps as you grow, you will change. Hell, I changed in my early forties."

Ted popped into Heather's mind, and she wasn't sure if she wanted to say something about it to Steve, something that would show vulnerability, something she never wanted to show. But, this was probably the best time to broach it. "I kind of know what you're talking about. Ted, well, he's a friend, but a bit more, and I'm not sure how I feel about him. He's not a sub, and I'm not sure I want him to be. Fuck, I'm not sure what I want him to be."

"I've been looking at this female led relationship thing, and I see that there are several levels. It seems you are at the highest level, but there are others where women take the lead, men follow, but it falls short of total domination. Perhaps there's a meeting ground for you two."

"Hum. I love total obedience, but maybe something a bit less. I'll have to think about that, and I don't want to talk to him about it unless I know where my cut off is."

"Life, my sweet girl, is about compromises. Each of you have a comfort level, and if you can both connect within that, perhaps there's a chance for you, happiness perhaps, but like anything, it's a gamble."

"Hell, Dad. I came here to give you advice, and you ended up giving me some, and I really appreciate it. I think these talks are good for both of us. By the way, I'm surprised Julie and Nadia are not out here."

"I'm not in the best mood, so I think they didn't

want to be around me and my toxic attitude."

"Well, I'll go see what Julie is up to. Perhaps we can study together in her room or something like that."

"Or you two can come out here. I'm half in the bag and ready for bed."

He got up and half stumbled into the master bedroom.

Heather knew that Julie wasn't particularly interested in Lisa and Steve's relationship, but as her best friend, she needed to talk.

"Julie, you can come out. Steve's gone to bed."

Wearing an old sweatshirt and pants, hair uncombed, Julie came out with a text book in her hand. "Yo, roomy, what's going on? What happened at your Mom's place?"

"She doesn't want to see Steve any more, at least for now. I'm afraid they will break up."

"No shit? Just because he couldn't get it up for her? Seems like over reacting to me."

"That whole mastectomy thing has gone down hard on her, and he just drove the point home. No boobs, no sex is how she put it."

"Never treat a man like an equal. That's my take."

"Well, Mom is all about equal relationships, even though I've seen that he almost always gives in to her."

"That's a start. So, what can we do?"

"I wish I knew. Hoping you had some ideas."

"Well, off the top of my head, she should give him an ultimatum."

"That would mean, if he couldn't do it, divorce, and I don't want to see my folks go that way."

"If they do, they both still care about you, and you can still live here and go back and forth."

"You can be so fucking dense Julie. It isn't about me and my living situation. I lost my first set of parents, shits that they were, but I love these two, and I want them to be happy together."

"Look, Heather. It's late and I'm beat studying for a test. Let me think about it for a few days. I'm there for my BFF. We'll put our two brilliant heads together and figure something out."

It was another night of staring up at the ceiling, worrying, until she finally fell asleep, waking in the morning no clearer than the night before. When Nadia came in for breakfast, Heather told her what was going on and asked if Nadia had any ideas.

"Plastic surgery. I've heard that they can get fat from other places and make realistic boobs, but I don't know how realistic."

"I don't know. I think she wants him to love her boobs or not."

Over coffee with Ted, Heather wasn't sure if she wanted to confide in him, as asking a man for advice was not her thing at all, but he'd always been sympathetic and willing to listen, so against her basic beliefs, she told him the story, asking him what he would do in that situation.

It was clear that he was uncomfortable discussing this subject, but with her sitting quietly, staring at him, he felt he had to come up with something. "Well, breasts are part of the turn on, but if it were me, I'd just turn out the lights and concentrate on other parts of her body. I think that would work, but I've never been in that situation."

Turning out the lights wasn't a bad idea, at least at first, until he got over this whole boobs thing. "Thanks Ted. You're a good friend."

"I'm here for you, friend or whatever you'd like." That was a brave gesture, knowing she would probably not respond. And she didn't react or comment. Just a friend. Well, that would do for now, maybe for always as much as he wished for something more.

Heather thought about what he'd said, a male perspective, and a possible starting point for dad. As she walked through campus, she realized that people were subtly avoiding her, and then she stopped and realized that she'd been wearing the same clothes for at least three days, hadn't combed her hair or done anything to remotely clean herself up. Worry about her mom had put the little details of life on the back burner. As she walked by a building, she looked at her reflection in the window. Damn, she thought, I've seen homeless people better kept than me. When's the last time you showered girl? Back in Santa Monica, days ago. Then she started to laugh. Ted was all friendly, and almost affectionate with this. She pointed at her reflection. The poor guy must have a thing for me. Too bad he's not a submissive.

With classes over and a half hour drive to Montecito, Heather arrived to find Steve reading the paper in the living room. "Hi dad. My friend Ted told me something today that may or may not help."

Steve looked up, expecting insights from his insightful girl. "And what was that?"

"Turn out all the lights. That way you don't see the lack of boobs, and then maybe you can get your mojo back."

"Well, we usually do it with at least one light on, but what the hell, assuming she even let's me near her again."

"I'll be talking to her. I'm not about to see my family fall apart." With that, Heather did something she rarely did, she started to cry, standing there feeling vulnerable, sad and like some fucking orphan.

That totally caught Steve by surprise. Heather hated to show any sign of weakness, and here she was looking broken. He got to his feet, went over to her, hugged her and said, "No matter what happens between me and your mom, we are now and will always be family. You have to believe me on that."

She looked into his eyes and realized he was deadly sincere, and she put her face against his chest and started the waterworks, the dam that had held back the tears for four years broken. She managed to say, through choking on the words, "Yes Dad, I believe you, and thank you for caring about your flawed daughter."

There it was, Heather admitting that she was flawed, but she wasn't really. She had learned to cope with situations that would have broken others, and in doing so, she had built a wall around her feelings. Her relationships were designed to never be an emotional threat, just casual, the men expendable. The girl had two close friends and this boy Ted, add him and Lisa, and that was it, the total of her social circle. Steve was reminded of how he'd been before meeting Lisa, a man with lots of acquaintances, but no real friends. He wanted to reach out to her, but he knew she wouldn't want anything unsolicited. This was a very proud young woman.

"Mom, I'll see you Friday evening after class." It was a mid-week call home.

"You can wait until Saturday. You know I'm fine now." There was a hint of impatience in her voice.

"I know, but I'm not, so I'm coming home after

class." She hoped she sounded adamant about this.

Heather realized she was spending less time with her friends these days, and this new distance was bothering her and apparently them also, but she had to focus on mom and dad and to try to save their marriage.

As always, as she passed Sage's place in Malibu, she considered stopping, perhaps using him for a few minutes, but as always, she was a woman on a mission, and she didn't want to waste time with some fucking guy, so she nodded in the direction of his little beach house as she drove by, wondering if he still hoped to hear from her. Well maybe one day when all this is taken care of.

"So, what brings my little girl here in such a hurry this weekend? Bored with your lovely place in Montecito or perhaps with that man who used to be my lover?"

"Mom. Please don't be that way. I had a long conversation with dad, and he's still crazy about you and broken hearted."

"He's a big boy, and he'll get over it. I'm thinking of giving up on men totally."

"Don't say that Mom. You are still a young woman, and I'm sure you still have urges."

"Well, urges can be resisted, and right now I have the urge for a cup of coffee. Join me?"

It was a warm spring day, so they took their coffee out on the patio with the soft sea breeze gently messing their hair, a small amount of beach haze keeping the sky from being a hard blue. Living less than a mile from the beach had its advantages. Lisa had bought this place when she first hired on as an assistant district attorney, and the high mortgage at the time seemed not much now, but she realized that home prices had gone up so fast that if she were to buy now, well, she couldn't buy this place. All her new neighbors were successful business executives with incomes of over a million per year. Her home, should she wish to sell, would go for close to two million bucks, four time what she paid. However, she loved Santa Monica, and she loved her job and the ability to walk on the beach any afternoon after work. Life was good, and she appreciated it all the more seeing that she almost died. Every day was now a new blessing, and she would take nothing for granted.

"You're smiling mom. What's up?"

"Just thinking how lucky I am, my job, my lovely daughter, my home. Life is good, and I don't need a man to keep it good."

"Even a good, loving man like dad?"

"Well, the jury is out on the good and loving stuff. You know my nipples used to be very erogenous zones, but they're gone along with my damn libido."

Mom, I don't believe you. I think you're still a raving horn dog, and you need Dad to keep you happy."

"Okay, my dear, what man do you need to keep you happy? I mean not just a casual sub for temporary pleasure, but actually happy."

She had her there. Heather didn't care about any men, except maybe Ted, but he was just a friend. No, Mom was right, a full time relationship with a man was of no interest to her. They were just fun when she had the time for them, which was not very often these days.

"We need to walk on the beach. When did we do that last?"

"Back when I was still sick, you and I and what's his name."

"Come on Mom. I want to feel the ocean between my toes and remember all the good times we've had."

Heather noticed that Mom was moving much more briskly this time, a sign that she was truly well, at least physically. Heather tried to imagine having scars where her breasts had been, wondering if she could still have subs under those circumstances. Male fantasies come in all types, but even subs have a thing about boobs. She has had many of them suck hers, and while they gave her loads of pleasure, they obviously enjoyed it themselves. Yes, no boobs, very likely no sex. Mom was wearing a padded bra, so fully dressed, she still looked quite sexy, and Heather hoped she would look that good over a quarter century from now.

"I love the beach. Walking in the sand seems to make me feel like an innocent kid again, makes me almost forget who I've been these last four years. Do you ever want to go back to being a kid again, just living for fun and letting your parents take care of all the shit?

"Actually, dear, I never look back. Life then was

okay, but I'm always hoping for awesome in the future, but unfortunately, awesome won't include a man, but I can adjust to that. After all, I didn't have a relationship for quite awhile before I met, well, you know.

"Come on Mom. Steve. Say his name."

"Okay, Steve the immature shit. That's who I'm talking about."

Heather looked up at the bluffs, remembering the poor boy, name somehow forgotten, that she'd pushed to his death. So much anger, and Mom had taken that angry girl and calmed her, making her, if not normal, at least not homicidal. Again, she tried to look to the future to middle age. Would she still be interested in continuing to be a dom, or would she give it up, perhaps find some other ways to live her life? Might she ever get married? That seemed the most far fetched idea of all. She would have to love one of her subs, and quite frankly none really seemed worth loving. They were just amusement for her, as she figured she was for them. A kinky sex life isn't a good fit with a long term loving relationship. Also, she really didn't think she could ever love a man. She loved her mom, perhaps Steve, and maybe Julie. She liked Nadia and Ted, but love, well that just didn't seem like anything she wanted. She pictured planning a mutual vacation, shopping for foods they both liked, even—god forbid—having kids, and none of it sounded the least bit desirable.

She looked over at her mom, a woman who seemed to have it all, and then it all went sideways, her health, her relationship, almost her career. She really couldn't imagine her life in twenty-five years, but then Mom's parents were retired but still alive and apparently enjoying themselves, but how could love last that long, beyond when a person's sex life was pretty much over. What's left to keep people together? Habit, she supposed, dull, predictable habit. When she got to Mom's age, Mom would be the age of her mom, a gray haired matron with memories of a once great love.

"Could we stop at My Goodness? I'd like to see Megan and have lunch."

"Lisa and Heather. Good to see you." Megan was in her black pants and sweater, waiting tables while her cook was busy in the back. "What's up?"

"Not much" said Lisa.

"Not true," said Heather. "Mom and Steve are estranged."

Lisa flashed her a sharp look, not wanting to share this information."

"What the fuck happened girl?"

"He failed me, and I don't want to talk about it."

Megan wasn't one to take no for an answer. "Shit girl. We're friends, business partners and a whole bunch more. Get it off you chest."

Heather put her arm around Lisa and said, "Please mom. Don't keep it all bottled up."

Lisa put her hands up to her face, rubbed her eyes and sighed. "Okay. They removed my breasts, and apparently Steve can't handle it, so he couldn't do it, and well, you can imagine how I felt."

Megan shook her head. "Don't give up on him girlfriend. Give him a little time to adjust. Men, well, they don't handle stuff very well. So, is he with you or in Montecito?"

"I sent him away. He's back in that big house."

Megan turned to Heather. "You stay there during the week?"

"Yeah, with three of my friends, all students."

"So, Heather, what does Steve say about this?"

"Says he loves her but feels sorry for her, and that well..."

"Keeps him from getting it up. Right?"

Lisa nodded an affirmation.

"Don't give up girlfriend. You two have a good thing, and with time he'll adjust."

Heather remembered what Ted had said. "My male friend said that if it were him, he'd just turn out the light and let his imagination do the work."

"Smart boy. We all cope in different ways. I remember how you didn't want to give in to the cancer or get help from your loving friends. We all get weird about different things."

Yeah, yeah. Everyone tells me the same thing, but it doesn't feel right. Maybe it will be okay some day, but for now, I just don't want to see him."

"Understood. Enjoy your breakfast, and I'll come by in a couple of days with a bottle of wine."

They ate in silence for a few minutes, and then Lisa admitted, "I didn't want her to know, but now, well, I'm glad you pushed it. I needed to talk about it."

Heather squeezed Lisa's hand and had a good feeling that she was doing something positive for her mom, something to help her as she had helped a very angry young girl.

Chapter 24

Nadia was home visiting her parents, so Heather invited her to lunch at a place a block from the beach. "How are you adjusting to college?"

"I like it much better than high school. Yet, there are so many submissive guys, it's hard to focus on my classes. I feel like a kid in a candy store."

"I was the same the first couple of months and then I realized that guys were like busses, miss one and another along in a few minutes. We will have our choice of guys for years, but only one chance to get a good education. Can you imagine having to depend on a man for support, to smile and laugh at his jokes and all the rest?"

"Yeah, we are hot, young and know how to handle guys. Life is good.'

"Getting along okay with Steve?"

"Oh yeah. He's a sweetheart. Still, he's become a real basket case because of that thing with your mom. I don't know what to say to him to, I don't know, make him feel better, give him advice, whatever."

"Don't worry about that. He's my project. I'm going to do whatever it takes to get them back together."

"You got your work cut out for you. Better you than me."

Driving home late Sunday afternoon, driving through Sage's neighborhood, again the urge to stop and play. This time she figured what the hell, an hour more or less, so she pulled over and called.

"Mistress Heather. I was afraid I wouldn't hear from you again. Where are you?"

"About a block from your place, and I'm horny and would like to stop by."

He was obviously anxious. "Oh yes, please do. Give me five minutes to clean stuff up."

She wanted to see if he remembered to be on his knees when greeting her, and sure as hell as soon as he opened the door, he dropped to his knees and told her how glad he was to see her. It's true, she thought, there are far more submissive guys out there than dominant women. He will do whatever I want in the chance to have a great orgasm.

"I'm feeling that I've neglected you far too long, so if you satisfy me, I will get you off in a way you won't soon forget." She dropped her pants and sat in a chair in his living room. He immediately started giving her oral sex, and she didn't realize how horny she'd been, exploding in just minutes. He deserved a reward for that, so she had him lie down on the bed, and she mounted him, already quite wet, moving up and down on him until he came with loud cries and seemingly unable to get his breath. "Thank you Mistress. That was wonderful."

"You've been a good boy, and you deserve it." This was perfect, only about a hour, and they were both satisfied. She put his head between her breasts and stroked his head, calling him a good, loyal sub. Then she said she had to get home, got dressed and left, noticing the disappointed look of a guy who was expecting more and not knowing when.

Wow, she thought, as she drove the last half hour to Montecito. I really needed that, and he is so obedient, which absolutely turns me on.

Julie, who rarely goes home to Santa Monica these days, was sitting in the living room, watching TV with a text book in her lap, trying to multitask, wearing a tank top, as she'd been doing for awhile, something that shows off her muscular build. She looked up as Heather walked in and remarked, "You look like you just got laid, big fucking smile, rosy cheeks."

"Yeah, finally stopped at Sage's place, and he was oh so happy to see me."

"I take it he was a good boy, took care of your needs."

"Yeah, is Nadia back yet?"

"Haven't seen her today."

"How about Steve?"

"I think he's in his room, or should I say, suite."

Heather walked down the hall to the master bedroom and knocked on the door.

"Yeah, who's there?
"Your brilliant daughter, Heather."
"I could use some brilliant, so come in."

He was sitting on a chair, near the fireplace, wearing sweats and listening to some seventies rock station turned down low, a magazine on his lap, hair disheveled, looking more like a middle aged man than ever. "Have a seat brilliant daughter and tell me how your mom is doing."

"She is still hurt from the whole pity thing. I think she will come around, but it's going to take time. What about you? You're still a good looking guy, rich, famous. Are you dating again?"

"No interest. I guess your mom has me locked up, and she's not mailing me the key. I really no longer want to have meaningless sex. Been there for years, and it's lost its appeal."

Heather quickly reflected on his comment, thinking that it wouldn't be that long before meaningless sex started to lose interest for her, but what then, a conventional, vanilla relationship. That to her would be even worse than years of meaningless sex. She wondered how it would be to have a female led relationship with just one loyal sub, a partner who would obey her and acknowledge her leadership. That might be an option, but for now quick sex with someone like Sage was quite enough. After all, men get in the way of a good education. If she ever did get into an exclusive relationship, she would want to be the most educated, highest earner. Having a man equal to her would not do it at all.

Turning her attention back to Steve, who was obviously distressed by his relationship on hiatus, she walked over to him, hugged him and said, "I'm working on her, and won't give up until she takes you back, but when she does, you better be ready to show some enthusiasm."

"Yes, you are my brilliant daughter, and if anyone can patch things up between us, it will be you."

Nadia didn't come home that night, and Julie and Heather were starting to worry. They called her parents, and were told they hadn't heard from her. Finally Julie called the highway patrol and gave them her license number and a description of the car, saying that she would be somewhere between Santa Monica and

Montecito. And no, she wasn't sure if she took the freeway or Highway One. Both of them had the same idea. What if she fell off the wagon, got someone to buy her booze and then who knows.

Later that afternoon, the highway patrol called. They found her. She had run off the road, crashed into a highway sign, fortunately no other car involved, but her blood alcohol level was twice the legal limit. She was in the emergency room at a hospital in Thousand Oaks and would be arrested when or if she was released.

When Heather got home, Julie filled her in. "Did they say if she was awake? If so, we should go see her."

"They didn't say, but I have the hospital's number, so let's find out."

The hospital told them she was still heavily sedated, and was being examined to determine the extent of her injuries, and no, not a good time to visit.

The next day in class it was obvious that something was bothering her, and when she went for coffee with Ted after class, it all came gushing out. She was afraid of losing a third of her total friends, Ted and Julie being the other two. Then she did something totally out of character, she started to cry, softly at first and then the dam broke. Nadia, Mom, Steve, and somehow it was all her fault, her inability to help those she loved.

Then he did something he'd always been afraid to do, he put his arm around her, and to his surprise, she leaned into him, her face in his chest, tears staining his shirt, and he just sat there until she calmed down.

Then after a few minutes she started to realize what she'd done, she sat up wiped her eyes and took a deep breath. "Sorry about that. That's not who I am."

"Please don't be sorry. That's what friends do, and you know I care about you."

She looked at him as if it were the first time, realizing how close they'd become, how he really did care for her, and for the first time she had a warm feeling for a guy, a good friend, a caring friend.

That night Julie told her the hospital promised to call as soon as Nadia could have visitors.

"As soon as they do, we'll go see her."

They realized that her absence from classes

would be a problem, so they went to the admissions department and told them Nadia had been in an accident, and probably wouldn't be in class for awhile, maybe the rest of the semester, and they said they'd wait a few days for more word before dropping her from her classes.

A couple days later, the hospital called and said they could visit, so Ted offered to drive and the three of them drove to Thousand Oaks and found a rather battered Nadia.

"How did this happen?"

"I stopped for some snacks, and some guy was hitting on me and offered to buy me some wine. He was cute, and I said what the hell, a bit of wine wouldn't hurt. Well, I planned to bring it home, but the traffic was bad, so I pulled over opened the bottle, unfortunately a screw top, a took a sip. Well, by the time I'd driven another forty miles, I'd killed the bottle and was pretty drunk. The rest is history. The cops are going to arrest me, and they wanted to know who bought it for me, but I only got the guy's first name, and I couldn't remember where I stopped, somewhere along 101 in the valley. But the worst is that there is some issue with my spine, and I'm waiting to hear from the doctor."

A few minutes later the doctor came in and asked the friends to step out for a minute. They were out in the hall when they heard a pitiful wail from her room, followed by sobbing.

When the doctor stepped out, they wanted to know what happened, and he said it would be better if they heard it from her. When they went in, Nadia was crying. "He doesn't think I'll ever walk again. My spine, something about L4, whatever the hell that is."

Ted had taken enough biology to know, and he said it was bad but could have been much worse. "As far as I can tell that's only going to affect your legs. The rest should work just fine."

"Just my legs! Just my fucking legs! Like I'm going to be in a wheelchair for the rest of my miserable life."

Julie, who was less than a sympathetic person, said, "At least you're alive. You could have killed yourself, and maybe taken others with you. You're barely eighteen, so they'll probably go easy on you, and he doesn't think you'll walk again, which isn't the same is saying that you'll never walk again. So, bad but not nearly as bad as it could have been."

"Yeah, sure, but my parents were so happy when I stopped drinking. I can't imagine how they'll handle this."

"You probably won't have to wait long." Ted was saying. "The cops have probably already told your parents, but maybe not, as you're not officially a minor any longer."

"Sure, I've been an adult for like three or four weeks; my first grown up act."

They check with the hospital staff as they were leaving and were told that the cops wanted to know when she'd be stable enough to be released. They were going to arrest her, but if she was paraplegic, they'd probably just take a report, fill out an arrest paper and let her go until her trial.

They said they were her roommates and would come for her when she was free to go.

"No wine for me tonight"

"Yeah Heather, I agree," said Ted.

"I guess it's me too." From Julie.

Heather was saying that she should have known, should have been there to help her friend.

Ted shook his head. "You are not responsible for everyone. Just be responsible for yourself. Nadia made a bad decision after months of sobriety, and it had nothing to do with you."

Heather hated to admit that a male was right, but Ted had a point she couldn't refute. She realized that she took on everything, made it personal, even though logically she couldn't possible influence most things.

Heather's foray into introspection was an uncomfortable trek for her, even though she was doing more of it lately. She had to ask herself what was the nature of her relationships with friends and family. Her circle was small, and perhaps that was why she worked so hard to maintain them, to maintain something like normal relationships.

The next day Julie received a call from the hospital. Nadia was out of danger, the police had booked her, and by tomorrow she would be able to be released. Did Julie want to pick her up, or should they call her parents. Julie asked to talk to Nadia to find out what she wanted, so they connected Julie to Nadia's room.

"They'll cut you loose tomorrow. Do you want to come here or to your parents?"

"What parents? As soon as they found out, they disowned me, calling me a hopeless drunk."

"Bad news. Okay, we'll come for you after classes tomorrow. Are you going to be able to keep going to school?"

"My parents paid up front for like three or four semesters, plus a scholarship. I'll be able to continue, and I guess I'll need that education. I'm no longer fit for physical work."

Heather was devastated to hear about Nadia being disowned, but Julie just told her to suck it up. "Not your fucking problem girlfriend."

They all agreed to go to the hospital the following day to make her feel loved and surrounded by friends, and they took Ted's car because it was big enough for four people and a wheelchair.

Nadia was glad to see her friends, and she told them that she now considered them her only family. Even her little sister had washed her hands of Nadia, and her grandparents were still in India, so they were out of the picture.

That night, Nadia in her new wheelchair, the others in overstuffed chairs. Steve, having heard about Nadia, came out and asked how she was, and found out about what her parents had done. "You kids have family here with me, and if there's anything I can do to help, just ask. Now, who has homework? All of you, right? Get busy. Dad's going to play hardball with you."

After he left the room, Nadia said, "God, I wish he were my real dad. Such a good guy."

Ted, looked at his watch and said, "Getting late. I'll turn in and read my assignment for tomorrow. Good night."

After he left the room, Julie ask Heather, "When are you going to fuck him? He's hot for you, and looks like you are hot for him."

"You know he doesn't want to be a part of our lifestyle, and I'm not into vanilla relationships. So, I guess not ever."

Then Nadia said, "Hell, just thinking about dominating guys. How the hell am I going to do that in one of these?"

"Well," Julie suggested, "There are guys for every conceivable kink, and I'm sure there are subs who get turned on by women in wheelchairs."

"Yeah, like about one in ten million."

After Nadia wheeled herself off to bed, Heather asked Julie what they could do to help her.

"First go to medical school, but until then all we can do is be positive and supportive. We can't fix her as much as we'd like to."

Now Heather had two problems to try to fix, Mom and Dad and Nadia. She was up early the following morning to join Steve for coffee. "How are you doing dad?"

"As well as can be expected. You know, now that Lisa and I are, how you say, estranged, I'm considering making another film. Saw a script I like, and it reminds me of my current situation. Acting helps put stuff in prospective, and I need something to do beside read and help you girls."

Heather didn't like the sound of that. "Does that mean you've given up on Mom?"

"Never, but until she's willing to talk to me, I have to just go on with my life."

"I want to ask you a question, and I want you to think about it and give me an honest answer. Okay?"

"Sure. Shoot."

"Do you think you can ignore her scarred body and be able to make love to her?"

"I think so. I hope so."

"When that becomes a definite yes, I'll help you patch things up, but please don't wait too long."

"You know I really want to do this. I love her. I'm just afraid that my body won't obey my desire when the time comes."

"Therapy dad. You can afford it, and maybe it will help."

"I'm willing to try, and thank you for your help."

That day in class, one of the male students approached her during the break, looking sheepish and uncomfortable. "Excuse me Heather. I've heard that you are a dominatrix. Is that true?"

"Yes, and why do you want to know?"

"Well, you see, I have a fantasy about being a

submissive, and I'm wondering, well, you know."

Heather looked him up and down, thinking he's not very interesting to look at, but normally she would at least have one session with him, but now, "Thanks for the offer, but this isn't a good time. I'll let you know if I change my mind."

The guy's downcast eyes gave her a slight thrill, as he nodded and walked away. What the hell is happening to me, she thought. I guess personal stuff has gotten in the way of my sex drive.

She had no idea why she decided to share this incident with Ted, but she couldn't stop herself from giving him an account of the interaction. He didn't say anything for a time, until her enquiring look seemed to ask for a response. "Well, from a male point of view, despite what many think, even men don't take every offer they get. If he doesn't do it for you, why would you bother."

That sort of made sense to her, but for some reason, she had to take it further. "So what do you think of something like that, I mean a guy offering to become a submissive?"

"Apparently there are guys out there who are into stuff like that. I can see it. I think I would prefer a female led relationship, but not with the kinky stuff. I think a woman should lead, and that a man should do whatever she needs for her satisfaction."

"Really, I didn't know that about you."

"I hadn't really thought about it until lately. I mean, I was thinking about a strong, leader type of woman, one who commands respect and all that, and I decided I like that type. I'm coming to the notion that women make good leaders. I think the foot worship and humiliation stuff is just over the top."

"I think that's considered FLR level one, which isn't too bad really."

For the first time Heather looked at Ted as a possible. Level one is a good place to start, and maybe she could move him to level two, which would be fun, and she would have a sub she actually liked, a friend and lover and if not a slave, at least a guy who would serve her needs. She decided not to push it any further at the moment.

Ted was also thinking that perhaps a relationship was possible, and he wondered how far he would be tempted to go with her. Having her take the lead in bed would be easy, as he wouldn't have to guess about what pleases her, and he already realized that a woman wouldn't stick around if she were not getting satisfied. Men are easy to satisfy, he thought, but women, far more complicated.

Steve was on it as far as therapy. Name recognition got him in within hours of calling. At his first session he came right to the point. "My wife had breast cancer, double mastectomy, and instead of passion I experienced pity or something like that and couldn't get it up. That hurt her, and she kicked me out. What can I do to get past this?"

The therapist, a woman, asked him a few more questions, and then made a few suggestions. "There is nothing wrong with having your eyes closed, many do it. Keep an image of how she looked the first time you made love, and then concentrate on all the other areas you love, neck, lips, ears, thighs, clit. Breasts are good, but there is so much more. Now, I want you to fantasize about her, at night, in the dark, on the bed. Get yourself aroused, but don't cum. Do this every night until you want her so bad you can hardly stand it. Then go to her, apologize for everything that you did to hurt her and beg for the right to make it up to her."

"Do you think that will work?"

"I think so, but this isn't rocket science. You have to make it work. You have to know that it might be your last chance with her. Do you absolutely love her?"

"Absolutely."

"Good. Do your homework tonight and see me again in the morning, around 9:30."

Steve did as the therapist suggested, in bed, in the dark, fantasizing. He was getting aroused, and then he pictured the scars where her breasts had been, and he felt his erection fade. More practice, he thought.

The following weekend, home with Lisa, Heather said Steve was getting therapy and was dedicated to saving the marriage. She reluctantly brought up the idea of breast reconstruction, and Lisa said she'd considered it. However, "I have to know he desires me first, and then, perhaps I'll get the reconstruction."

That night Megan came by with a bottle of wine.

She was underage the first time they'd met, and now, in her early twenties, she was a serious entrepreneur and a strong, assertive woman, someone Heather admired. Mom and Megan were two role models for her, two women who stood on their own two feet and didn't put up with crap from men or from anyone else.

Chapter 25

Remembering Nadia's situation, Heather only had one glass of wine, not wanting to be tempted to over do it, to slip into alcoholism. One drink; two maximum. She noticed that both women sipped their wine slowly, making a glass last the better part of an hour, so they could make two glasses last the evening. Role models indeed.

When she got back to Montecito, she asked Steve how therapy was going. He'd been to see the therapist four times and felt he was making progress. She didn't say anything about the reconstruction, mostly because she wanted him to get over this on his own, to own the fact that his wife was the same woman, boobs or not.

"It's odd to talk to you about this, you know, dad to daughter, but okay, I've gotten to the point where I can fantasize about her, even picture her scarred and still, well, keep it up."

"Good for you dad. I hope you two can get it back together soon. Worrying about you two is hurting my grades."

"I'm not going to be happy if you fail any classes. I was an A student, and so was your mom, so high expectations.

Heather was amazed at how observant Ted was. The first thing he said is, "You look more relaxed, less stressed and anxious. Are things improving with your parents?"

That touched her. She'd never known a male like him before, and she was beginning to think of him as more than a friend, less than a possible sub, but those were the only two options in her mind. Female led relationship level one she thought. Yes, that might do very well. She took his hand and said, "Yes they are, and to celebrate, I'm going to take you to dinner tonight, a nice place near the Santa Barbara Harbor, my treat, and no argument."

"Thank you. I'd love that."

The sun was starting to set as they sat down at the restaurant at a west facing table. "Order anything you'd like, and don't pay attention to the price."

Easy to say, he thought, but being a man, he was uncomfortable with a woman spending a lot of money on him, so he ended up with something in the mid price range, the meal not mattering as much as the company. He was wondering if she had anything else in mind, and the thought made him a bit anxious. He'd been with girls before, but teen sex, spontaneous fucking. This girl, no woman, was a different matter, someone who would call the shots, instruct him on what to do and how to do it. Would he be able to handle that, or would his insecurities cripple his libido. But, what the hell, she may not have anything like that in mind, so he told himself, just enjoy your meal dummy.

She talked about Lisa and Steve, and how Steve was going to a therapist, and Ted should not let him know that she talked about it, and perhaps if things went well, mom would have breast reconstruction, and perhaps their marriage would be saved, and maybe Nadia would walk again one day, and everything would be the way it was meant to be.

Ted listened carefully, attentively and without interrupting. Amazed at the uncharacteristic vulnerability she was showing, knowing that if anything would burst this moment, it might never come again.

She suddenly came out of the reverie she seemed to be in and abruptly stopped. "Thanks for listening to me. Guess I had a lot on my mind. Hope I didn't get too carried away."

"Not at all. I hope it all comes true for you and your family."

Sitting with coffee as the last light faded, and the sky went from yellow to red to purple, they didn't speak for some time, looking out the window, lost in thought.

Now, looking out at the night sky, Heather asked for the bill, and Ted tried to catch a look at it, to see how much, but Heather paid and quickly got up. They drove back to Montecito, a short drive, pretty much in silence.

No one was in the living room, which made Ted feel a bit more relaxed. They sat down facing each other, Heather staring at him, as if trying to decide what to do with him. "Ted, I'm thinking of taking you to bed. How does that sound to you?"

"Exciting, but a bit intimidating, to be honest."

"That's good. Intimidating men excites me. Do you think you could or would give me oral sex? Do you even enjoy that?"

"Yes and yes I do enjoy it. Do you mean now?"

"I think now would be a good time. Let's go to my room."

Ted was nervous, knowing that he had one chance to make the right sexual impression, that Heather would not abide bad sex. He was actually glad she suggested oral sex, as he was so nervous that he didn't think he could perform.

They went into her room, and she left the light on. "I would like you to undress for me. Would you be okay with that?"

Ted's heart was racing. "Yes, Heather, I will do that." He started peeling off his clothes, trying to make it look sexy. First his shirt, then pants, tee shirt and underwear, and he was pleased to find he had a partial erection. She stood quietly as he did this, watching him and smiling. Finally she walked up to him, ran her hands over his shoulders and chest, gently stroked his cock and said, "You are a sexy boy. Would you like to see me naked?"

He managed to say yes, and she started to strip for him, making his cock become even more erect. Finally, she lay back on the bed, legs spread and motioned for him to come closer. He kneeled down at the foot of the bed, ran his tongue up and down the inside of her thighs until she pulled his head closer. Then he found her clit with his tongue and went to work to bring her to orgasm, and it didn't take very long.

"Oh, yes, that was so good. Would you like me to fuck you?"

"Yes."

"It would be better if you could say yes Mistress. Can you do that?"

He wanted it bad by then, so "Yes Mistress."

She got up and had him lie down where she had been, and then she climbed up on the bed, stroked his cock until he felt he was almost ready to cum, and then she sat down on him, putting him into her. "Don't cum yet." Then she started moving up and down on him, slowly at first, picking up speed. Then they both had an orgasm at the same time, and Ted knew he'd had the experience of his life.

Heather got off him and kneeled down on the bed beside him, studying him closely. He asked what she was thinking, and she said, "Usually I end it at this point, but I'm thinking of having you stay the night. Would you like to do that?"

"Yes, I would love that."

"Okay, so if you'll go into my bathroom and get a washcloth and clean us up."

He was totally hooked, and possibly in love. So he got up, found the washcloth, poured warm water on it, wrung it out and came back, first cleaning her up and then himself. After tossing the washcloth in the hamper, he climbed back in bed next to her.

"I would love to hold you and cuddle you if that's okay."

This was unfamiliar territory with her, so she had to think about it for a moment, but then the idea started to feel good, warm and fuzzy as they say. "Yes, that would be nice."

They feel asleep in each other's arms.

Heather woke up first, looked over at Ted and thought that somehow she had crossed a line she'd never intended to cross, but one that felt good. I can always backtrack, she thought, but for now, I'll enjoy this sweet boy. He looks so peaceful lying there. It wasn't all I usually want from a guy, but it was quite satisfying, and with time he will get even better.

Then she had the urge to do something completely out of character. She bent over and kissed his forehead, waking him up. As soon as his eyes opened, seeing her close, he smiled. "Good morning Heather, or is it Mistress Heather?"

"Heather is fine for now."

"Okay, I would love to fix breakfast for us."

"Oh, yes. That sounds very nice."

Over breakfast he asked about the status of the relationship, hoping they were now a couple. She assured him that she liked him and was willing to continue, but, she warned, long term commitments were not her thing, and they would just take it as it comes. She wanted to know if he could live with that.

He wanted to say anything to be with you, but he used some restraint. "Yes, Heather, I can live with that. No pressure, no relationship talk."

Julie came in wearing panties and a bra, seemingly unconcerned about her appearance, took a long look that them and said, "Someone has been doing some serious fucking."

Ted was too embarrassed to answer, but Heather said, "Indeed, serious fucking. Where's Nadia?"

"She got up early. School has a disabled transport, and they picked her up for class."

"Great. I was afraid she'd have to drop out for the semester."

Apparently Steve had also left early, probably another therapy appointment. Heather would ask him about it that evening. As for now, she and Ted had a ten o'clock class, and he said, "Why don't I drive. No sense taking two cars."

That evening, Steve was stretched out on the eight foot sofa, glass of wine in one hand, script for upcoming film in the other. "How was school Heather?"

"Same old same old. How are things going in your therapy sessions?"

"Great. She has be visualizing Lisa, scars and all and getting turned on by her, and it seems to be working. I think I can do this, but how to convince her to let me get close. I figure that's where you come in."

"Great. I'll be headed down this weekend, and I'll do whatever I can to convince her. I so much want my family back together. Is that the new film? Mind if I have a look?"

He handed it to her, and she sat down and started scanning. His character was a traumatized middle aged man who had been in Desert Storm and was suffering from PTSD, a serious role, nothing like the stuff that made him famous. "Heavy stuff Dad, I can't wait to see it."

"And you'll give me your honest opinion as to how convincing I am in the role?"

"Absolutely. I'm nothing if not brutally honest."

Later that evening Ted had the chance to catch Steve alone, and he wanted some romantic advice.

"Steve, I think Heather and I have started something, and any advice you can give me would be appreciated."

"Sure, but first, how do you feel about my sweet daughter?"

"I think I'm in love with her, but I don't think she feels the same way."

"That's a real stretch for her. My advice is to be really patient. Don't try to push a relationship. Let her come around to deciding how she feels. I get the impression she likes you more than anyone she's known, but if you start talking about love, she'll run. Be supportive. Try to please her, and pay attention to what she says and how she acts. If you can win her over, you'll have a really fine woman, but if you hurt her, well remember my film, Revenge of the Brothers."

Ted laughed at the thought of Steve letting loose with an assault rifle.

The next two nights Heather didn't invite Ted to her bed, and he was smart enough not to ask. Friday afternoon she would be driving down to Santa Monica, so he wouldn't see her until Sunday evening, and he was already missing her just thinking about it. I've got it bad, he was thinking.

Friday, Heather could hardly wait to get home to see her mom, passing by Sage's place without giving him a thought. He was as good as forgotten.

"Mom, Steve has been in therapy, and he's ready to make it up to you. I so hope you will give him another chance."

"I don't know. I don't want to think about another session like that. Made me feel less of a woman, and that really hurt."

"Sometime you just have to take a chance and risk being hurt. I know how scary that is."

Lisa laughed. "This from a girl who has layers of emotional protection all around her."

"Not so much anymore. I had Ted spend the night, and it felt good, almost right, and I've never felt like that. It is kind of scary, opening myself up emotionally and all that shit."

"Tell me all about it, and I'll try to give you some advice."

Heather related the entire story, the dinner date, having him undress for her, undressing for him, sex that she instigated and the cuddling after along with the waking up with him and how that felt.

"It sounds like you might have a boyfriend. Is that a scary thought?"

"I know you are joking with me, but actually it is a scary thought. I don't really want or need a boyfriend."

"You may not need one, but the wanting part, well, that remains to be seen."

"I don't want to get emotionally involved with him or anyone."

"It seems you already are to some extent. My advice is to see where it goes, stay in control and if it isn't comfortable, end it."

"I'll take your advice, but you also need to take mine. Just see him once, and if you aren't happy, you can push him out of your life. Really Mom, this is important to me, to Steve and to you."

"Okay, I'll give him one shot, and see how it goes. Tell him to call me and we can set up a visit or something. That's as big a commitment as I can make."

Heather jumped up, rushed over and gave Lisa a big hug. "Thank you mom."

To show her appreciation, Heather got busy in the kitchen, making a big meal for the two of them, telling Lisa that she neither needed or wanted any help.

When Heather got back to Montecito Sunday evening, Steve was still reading his script, probably had been trying out his lines. It was good to see him working again, rather than sitting around in old sweats and slippers.

"Dad, have a minute?"

Steve put down his script and looked up at her as she stood in the middle of the room. He just nodded.

"Mom said you should call her, and then maybe she'll invite you to come over. Maybe she's getting horny and could use some attention." She smiled at the thought.

Without a word, Steve grabbed his phone and called. "Hi Lisa, my love. Heather said you'd like to talk to me."

"We have some issues to settle. Would you like to come over?"

"Name the day and time, and I'll there. Doing nothing here but reading a new script."

"You can tell me about it when you see me. Is

tomorrow too soon?"

Steve almost shouted yes in the phone, so it was a go. Heather didn't really need his two thumbs up.

He got up, and Heather hugged him and told him not to blow this. She was feeling happy, knowing she was putting her family back together again.

"Busy day at school tomorrow, so good night Dad."

"Good night. Ted looked kind of sad this weekend. I guess he missed you."

Stretched out on the bed, Heather thought about Ted, and yes he seemed to be rather taken with her, but did she really want to pursue this. He was a nice guy, but if they developed a relationship, that would mean less time for other sexual adventures with all the potential subs roaming around campus, hoping to find a dom like her. Maybe it would even become exclusive, which frankly scared the shit out of her.

Chapter 26

They drove to school again on Monday, which made sense since their schedules were almost the same, and gas was expensive, and they could take turns driving, and it all sounded so logical, but there was obviously more to it.

"How did it go with your mom?"

"Steve will be heading down there this afternoon when Mom gets off work. If he doesn't screw it up, they'll be back together."

Ted smiled and shook his head. "That's the way it goes. Men have to be careful not to screw it up and lose the woman. It's pretty hard for a woman to screw it up. If the guy is already into her, she can do lots of shit and he'll let it go."

"Yeah, I guess it's a woman's world. Would you have it any other way?"

"Not really. I like having a woman keep me on my toes."

"Really Ted. Am I keeping you on your toes?"

"That should be obvious. You notice I'm not asking, pushing or even suggesting anything. Just chilling and waiting for you to send a signal."

That touched something in her that felt good. "How about this for a signal. How would you like to spend the night with me tonight?"

"I think you know my answer."

"You know that you are being so easy. Aren't you going to play hard to get?"

Ted laughed. "I'm about as hard to get as those cookies on the kitchen table. What can I say, you clearly call the shots."

"Yes, and that really matters."

Ted thought about that. This is and will be a female led relationship, but she isn't asking for the kinky stuff, and he really likes having her take the lead in bed. That way no guesses as how to please her, and pleasing her pleases him. He had been reading about this whole FLR stuff, and there was much about limits and respecting those limits, and it seems like she could do that. He didn't know what he'd do if she wanted him to kiss her feet or something like that. Still she knows his limits. They discussed it, and she still asked him to spend the night, so hopefully this was headed in the right direction.

"How do you feel about me?" That came out of the blue from her, and he wasn't sure how to respond.

"I like you and care about you and enjoy being with you and around you."

"Are you in love with me?"

Damn, how to answer that. It's kind of like the "do you still beat your wife" question. He decided to be as honest as he could. "I think so, but it's like early in this whatever we have, so hard to be sure and all that."

He was stammering, and probably embarrassing himself.

"I had a guy in love with me once. That stupid lawyer Timmy who kept me out of jail. But I had absolutely no respect for him."

"I hope you respect me."

"Yeah, I do. You're a good guy, and I like you."

Ted had a hard time concentrating on his classes, anticipation getting to his imagination. He remembered how exciting it was to strip in front of her and have her inspect him, slap him on the ass and play with his cock. He felt like a sex object, and that was rather exciting.

That night they did the gratuitous socializing with Julie and Nadia before excusing themselves and heading to her room. Julie's smirk made him just a bit uncomfortable. "Good night you two horn dogs."

That night was almost like the first one, with a few sexy additions. He was surprised at how she could get them to the point where they climaxed together, which was incredible. Then he put his head between her warm, soft boobs and fell asleep, waking up only with the sun coming in the window, Heather sitting up in bed watching him.

"How long have you been awake, you know, like

this?"

"A few minutes. I was enjoying watching you sleeping like a baby. I guess sex really relaxes you."

Ted had no idea when or if she would invite him to her bed again, so he could only wait and hope. She was so hot, such a sexual wonder. Did he love her? Hell yes.

Steve didn't return that day or the next, so Heather figured things were working out. She really wanted to call, but that might mess up whatever was going on, so she decided to just wait, even though the waiting was killing her as her imagination was on overdrive. Nervous about what was going on, she invited Ted to bed again, thinking good sex would relax her and make her sleep, which it did.

Two nights in a row. She shouldn't do it three in a row. That would be too much like a relationship, a dirty word if every there was one. She was resolved to put it on hold for at least another week, but when Ted got up, yawned and said good night, she felt insulted. "Wait just a minute. Are you going to leave me unfulfilled and horny? Shame on you. Now you just get yourself into my bedroom and get ready to get fucked."

She woke early the next morning, upset with herself. Damn, she thought, I did it again. Three nights in a row is bad news, but maybe it's just so I don't keep thinking about Mom and Steve. Yeah, Ted is keeping my mind off things, and when I find out how it went, I won't need to do this every night. He probably thinks we are in a relationship, which we absolutely are not.

It seemed forever, but it was only four days when Steve pulled into the driveway. Heather ran out to meet him just as the sun was setting. "What happened? Are you and Mom back together?"

"Slow down anxious daughter. Give me a chance to get in the house, use the bathroom and pour a glass of wine." It was obvious he was enjoying keeping her in suspense.

To a woman like Heather, having to wait was almost unthinkable, but since it was dad, she would have to hide her impatience and wait until he was ready, but one look at him told her that it went well. She followed him in the house. Julie, Nadia and Ted were in the living room, each with a text book in front of them. Steve motioned Heather to follow him into the library, and then he shut the door. "We're good."

"Come on dad. That's not information. Tell me all."

"We made wonderful love several times, and I told her I loved her. Actually, I told her that quite often. We went to dinner, talked, sipped wine, laughed, took walks and all that. Then the UFO landed, and she was abducted."

That caught Heather by surprise. "What!"

"Just seeing if you were paying attention. Everything was perfect, and she asked me if she should get a breast reconstruction, and I said it was totally up to her and that I love her however. Then she said she was going to get the operation, as if she wouldn't do it if it mattered to me. Go figure."

"She was testing you."

"You think?" Steve laughed. "Anyway, all is good, and now you have two loving parents who care about your school work. Now, your turn. What's going on with you?"

She told him about taking Ted to bed three nights in a row, but that now that she didn't have to worry about Mom, she wouldn't be doing that any more.

"I don't believe you. My little girl has a boyfriend, whether you wanted one or not. You did manage to pick a good one. Don't drive him away."

Heather was determined to not let Ted become her boyfriend, so she ignored him as best she could, driving to school by herself and not inviting him to bed. He was obviously disappointed, but to his credit, he hid it very well, always being friendly and cordial. Their after class coffee was an established ritual, one that wasn't likely to be broken. However, the coffee chat was about class and nothing about the personal relationship. This lasted for over two weeks, while Steve made repeated trips to Santa Monica, and Nadia found she could move one leg just a little bit, giving her hope for recovery.

Heather decided to have fun with one of the subs she'd had at school, a guy she hadn't seen in weeks, and she hoped to have the usual exciting kinky sex, but it turned out to be a big disappointment. She actually thought about Ted, as the guy was giving her oral sex.

Heather had an iron-clad image of herself, one she'd been building since her fifteenth birthday, and she was determined to not let anyone diminish it, particularly some damn male. So, her urge to take Ted to bed was countered by the need to maintain her self-image.

She was sitting at her desk in her bedroom, looking at the phone numbers of the subs she had enjoyed at school, trying to decide who to call. Unable to make up her mind, she gave up and went back to studying for her upcoming biology test. However she ran into something she was unsure of, and as much as she didn't want to, she knocked on Ted's door out by the pool.

He answered the door, looking like a puppy who was about to be taken for a walk. "Yes, Heather, what is it?"

"There's something I don't understand about the Nuclear matrix." He cocked his head and thought about it for a moment before inviting her in.

"I think I understand it. Have a seat, and let's discuss it."

They sat and talked for over an hour, until they agreed that they both understood. Then she thanked him and left his room.

As soon as she walked out, she started thinking about the great sex she'd had with him, trying to justify both her interest in him and her desire to not become involved. This was getting in the way of her life, her self-image and her sense of total independence. He's just a male, and there are plenty out there just as good in bed, as good looking or more, as interesting... No, none of them were as interesting as Ted, and none of them understood her as he did. That night she did something she considered taboo, she dreamed about him, not just sexually but in other ways. She hated the fact that women seemed to need men, and that could lead to getting emotionally involved. She also hated that life was becoming more complicated.

Then, he didn't come to the main house one morning for the usual breakfast, so she went to his room and knocked. "You okay in there Ted?"

"I think I've got the flu. Tell the professor I'm sick and won't be in class."

"What about breakfast?"

"I can't get out of bed, so I'll skip it today."

"No, you need to eat. I'll fix you something."

She made him a breakfast, eggs, ham, potatoes and fruit, brought it to him on a tray and had him sit up to eat in bed. He thanked her profusely, saying she shouldn't bother.

"Nonsense. I'm not going to let my... She was going to say boyfriend, but changed it to friend... go hungry. Eat, and if you have homework to turn in, give it to me and don't argue with me. I'm your nurse while you're sick, and I give the orders."

"Yes Mistress Heather. Whatever you say. I'm at your mercy."

Why did he have to say that? He was pushing her buttons, being dependent on her, giving her his power, something that was a sexual and emotional turn on for her.

The next day he was feeling somewhat better, well enough to go to class, but Heather had to take his temperature first, finding it normal. Then she said he could go, but she would drive. She bundled him up, got him in the car and drove him to school.

Then she took care of him for a few days until he was well. In the process, she started to feel he was her charge, and that he had to listen to her advice on his health, something he was willing to do, partly because her advice made sense and partly because he could see that they were becoming closer.

Finally, after a few more days she asked him if he were well enough for sex, which as a guy, the answer is almost always yes. After they finished, and she had not said anything about staying, he got up and started to dress.

"No you don't. Get back in bed. I need some cuddling." She could hardly believe she'd said "cuddling." This wasn't her at all. He climbed back in bed and wrapped his arms around her, telling her how special she was. He was obviously totally devoted to her, and as this sank in, as he held her, running his face through her hair, she stepped over the red line she'd drawn at fourteen. "You need to understand that you are my boyfriend now. You date only me, and you don't look at other women."

"If I'm your boyfriend, how could I even dream of looking at another woman. But you know the kinky stuff, foot worship, bondage, whips and all that doesn't work for me, so I hope you can live with that."

"How about pegging. I do have a nice strapon I'd like to use on you."

"That sounds weird, so I don't know."

"Read about it. Some men have really strong orgasms that way, and I'd like you to try, maybe liking it, but if you don't, say stop, and I'll understand.'

"Okay, I'm willing to try."

That was all it took. She jumped up, found the strapon, strapped in on and told him to roll over. Then she used lots of lube, realizing that it was his first time, slowly inserted it, hearing him gasp in pleasure, and she gradually pushed harder and deeper until he had an orgasm.

"Did my Teddy boy like that?"

"OMG yes. I had no idea."

"Then we can make that part of our sexual activity?"

"Yes Heather. Absolutely."

Two days later, Nadia returned from the doctor, and she was obviously excited. Julie asked what had happened, and Nadia said that there was some sensation in one leg, and that it was possible that she may walk again some day, with lots of therapy. He'd also said that she would likely never get back to her pre accident mobility, but walking with crutches or a cane was possible.

Things had been happening so fast that Heather had almost forgotten that her nineteenth birthday was fast approaching. She hadn't thought about it until Lisa called to say that she and Steve were going to take her out to whatever place she wished, and she immediately thought of the place she'd taken Ted on their first date, and she asked if Ted could come along.

"Naturally, you can invite him. Sounds like you have a relationship now."

It took her a moment to catch her breath and admit, "Yes, he's my boyfriend, and I would love to have him celebrate with us."

Sitting in the restaurant, looking out the window at the setting sun, surrounded by her family and her boyfriend, Heather felt she'd somehow come full circle, and that life was good, was rich and, despite being flawed, she was grateful for her awesome luck.

Other books by Meade Fischer

Cosmic Coastal Chronicle:A solitary wanderer travels the west coast from Big Sur to British Columbia. searching for surf, kayaking spots, hiking trails, interesting people and some insights into the great mysteries of life. Lost in a world of peace and beauty, he both celebrates and learns the lessons of life. (non fiction)

Shattering the Crystal Face of God: A spiritual cynic searches for personal truth and meaning in encounters with nature and the lessons of the spontaneous. (non fiction)

Spinning Real Life: In this satire, an idealistic young writer- sets out to write about real life and gets hopelessly emeshed in it, as world-changing events unfold around him and the women in his life are always one step ahead of him. (fiction)

Messiah Chronicles: The Jesus story, sans the miracles.A religious reformer, with his band of followers, travels ancient Judea, preaching religious reform, which angers some segments of his society.A Roman centurian takes a liking to hi- mand tries to protect him, while keeping the peace.

Clueless Guy's Guide to Love and Beyond: A humorous take on self help books, written for the clueless guys and the women how love them and laugh at them.

Her Grand Plan: A young girl's seven year plan for a literary career and an obsession to marry her mentor and teacher, and her attempt to get him to share her vision.

A *California Exploer:* five years of hiking stories in Califonria Explorer

The Boy from Tomorrow: a boy from the future learns to cope with the primitive 21st century.

Clueless Guy's Guide to Love and Beyond: A humorous take on self help books for the clueless guys and the women who laugh at them.

To Sea for Myself:Reflections of a Solitary Kayaker: Kayaking alone on the west coast of the US and Canada.

Shadows in the Forest: Bigfoot, space travelers hiding in the redwood forests, hoping for rescue, Pursued, trapped light years from home.

Beyond the Veil: Conversations with the non-material self: During a stressful time, a man connects with his non-material self and learn lessons about life, time and reality.

Flawd! A 14 year old girl kills three boys on first dates, but is so adorable she isn't convicted. The prosecutor ends up adopting her and reforming her. She finally learns about her dominant personality.

www.meadefischer.com
Or, search for Meade Fischer on amazon.com

www.ingramcontent.com/pod-product-compliance
Lightning Source LLC
LaVergne TN
LVHW021816060526
838201LV00058B/3414